Kurt Vonnegut was born in  biochemistry at Cornell Univer
he served in Europe and as
witnessed the destruction of
from this profoundly disturbing exp
novel *Slaughterhouse-Five*, arose, which lifted him
rank of contemporary American novelists.

After the war, he specialized in anthropology at the University of Chicago before turning to full-time freelance writing. His earlier books were mainly science-fiction with which he achieved considerable success and his first book *Player Piano* (1952) has been hailed as a major SF anti-utopian novel. Although he has since declared to have abandoned the science-fiction genre, there are still strong elements of this particular style of imaginative writing in his books.

Graham Greene has called him 'one of the best living American writers' and no matter what type of fiction Vonnegut claims to be writing, his commitment to humanity and his special concern for its more fallible specimens illumines all his work.

By the same author

Player Piano
The Sirens of Titan
Canary in the Cathouse
Mother Night
Cat's Cradle
God Bless You, Mr Rosewater
Welcome to the Monkeyhouse
Slaughterhouse-Five
Breakfast of Champions
Slapstick or Lonesome No More!
Between Time and Timbuktu
Wampeters, Foma and Granfalloons
Jailbird

Jan

Kurt Vonnegut

Happy Birthday,
Wanda June

A PANTHER BOOK

GRANADA
London Toronto Sydney New York

Published by Granada Publishing Limited in 1975
Reprinted 1976, 1979, 1981

ISBN 0 586 03921 X

First published in Great Britain by
Jonathan Cape Ltd 1973
Copyright © Kurt Vonnegut, Jr. 1970, 1971

Granada Publishing Limited
Frogmore, St Albans, Herts AL2 2NF
and
36 Golden Square, London W1R 4AH
866 United Nations Plaza, New York, NY 10017, USA
117 York Street, Sydney, NSW 2000, Australia
100 Skyway Avenue, Rexdale, Ontario, M9W 3A6, Canada
61 Beach Road, Auckland, New Zealand

Set, printed and bound in Great Britain by
Cox & Wyman Ltd, Reading
Set in Linotype Pilgrim

Granada ®
Granada Publishing ®

ABOUT THIS PLAY

This play is what I did when I was forty-seven years old –
when my six children were children no more. It was a time
of change, of goodbye and goodbye and goodbye. My big
house was becoming a museum of vanished childhoods –
of my vanished young manhood as well.

This was on Cape Cod. There were widows all around
me – in houses like mine.

I was drinking more and arguing a lot, and I had to get
out of that house.

I was supposedly a right-handed person, but I found
myself using my left hand more and more. It became the
hand that did most of the giving and taking for me. I
asked my older brother what he knew about this. He said
that I had been an ambidextrous infant. I had been *taught*
to favour my right hand.

'I'm left-handed now, and I'm through with novels,' I
told him. 'I'm writing a play. It's plays from now on.'

I was writing myself a new family and a new early
manhood. I was going to fool myself, and spooks in a
novel couldn't do the job. I had to hire actors – pay them
to say what I wished them to say, to dress as I wished
them to dress, to laugh, to cry, to come or go when I said
to.

Strictly speaking, I was rewriting an old play of mine.
But that old play had been written by a right-handed
stranger fifteen years my junior.

Fifteen years ago my wife and I conducted a Great Books
programme on Cape Cod. And when we read and

discussed *The Odyssey*, the behaviour of Odysseus at his homecoming struck me as cruelly preposterous. So I wrote a play about it, which I called *Penelope*.

Ernest Hemingway was still alive and seemingly well. So I felt free to imagine a modern Odysseus who was a lot like that part of Hemingway which I detested – the slayer of nearly extinct animals which meant no harm.

The play was performed for one week at the Orleans Arena Theatre on the Cape. Harold Ryan, the hero, had a line in that version which went like this: 'Things die. All things die.' After the play closed at Orleans, I said that to my wife, and I returned to writing short stories and novels.

As a footnote to American theatrical history: the Orleans Arena Theatre, run by Gordon and Betsy Argo, produced six new plays by unknown writers, with no financial help from anyone.

During that same year, the Ford Foundation underwrote the production of ten new plays – at a cost of a hundred thousand dollars or more.

The Argos lost something like three hundred and nineteen dollars that year. So it goes.

*

Penelope, which became *Happy Birthday, Wanda June*, has been around so long that it was once optioned by Estelle Parsons – before she decided to be an actress. Think of that. Estelle used to suppose that she would be a producer some day.

She failed to produce *Penelope* for this reason: it was a lousy play. Actors complained that there were no parts for stars, that everybody got to talk as much as everybody else, that nobody changed or was proved right or wrong at the end.

This intolerable balancing of characters and arguments reflected my true feelings: I felt and I still feel that everybody is right, no matter what he says. I had, in fact, written a book about everybody's being right all the time, *The Sirens of Titan*. And I gave a name in that book to a mathematical point where all opinions, no matter how contradictory, harmonized. I called it a *chrono-synclastic infundibulum*.

I live in one.

Somewhere in there my father died, and one of the last things he said to me was that I had never written a story with a villain in it. That was surely one of the troubles with my play – and that remains a major trouble with it to this day. Even after we opened *Happy Birthday, Wanda June*, we experimented shamelessly with endings. We had various people shoot Harold, including children. We had Harold shoot various people, including children. We had Harold do the world the favour of shooting himself.

Nothing satisfied, and I am persuaded that nothing could satisfy, since the author did not have the balls to make Harold or anybody thoroughly vile.

That was chickenhearted of me. It was Edgar Lee Masters' *Spoon River Anthology*, and some other things, which has made me chickenhearted about villainy. I marvelled at all the epitaphs in Masters' book when I was only twelve years old, and I was bound to say to myself, 'My gosh – all those people *had* to be what they were.'

My father and mother also tended to make me chickenhearted. My father was a frail architect and painter. He was also a gun nut, which used to amaze me. It seemed so inharmonious with the rest of him, that he should fondle guns.

He left me some guns.

My two siblings didn't like his gunplay, either. One time, I remember, my brother looked at a quail Father had shot, and he said, 'My gosh – that's like smashing a fine Swiss watch.' My sister used to cry and refuse to eat when Father brought home game.

Some homecoming for Odysseus!

Lester Goldsmith produced my play. He had never produced a play before. He used to be an executive at Paramount Pictures. And then he became an independent producer of political films. We met in the spring of 1970, at the home of Don Farber, who was a lawyer for both of us.

Lester remembered having read a synopsis of *Penelope*, which my agents had circulated around Hollywood years before. After we'd all had a few drinks, he said, 'I'll option that play.'

Which he did. And I went home and rewrote it all summer long.

Lester and I were inspired amateurs where legitimate theatre was concerned. We remain good friends. God willing, we'll produce more plays less amateurishly.

Lester hired a theatre before we had a script. And he moved so quickly that we needed a director almost immediately. No New York director was willing to take the job without a finished script in hand. What I had to show at that point, two months before opening night, was a filthy tossed salad of corrasable bond.

A television director from the West Coast examined the tossed salad. He was a good man who had directed such gruesome enterprises as *Gilligan's Island* and *The Art Linkletter Show*. He had done a lot of little theatre, too, and had as his happiest memories the days when he had been the director of the road company of *Mr Roberts*. His name was Michael J. Kane.

Mike and I must have come within a few hundred yards of each other in 1949 or so, when I saw his production of *Mr Roberts* in Schenectady, New York. I was a public relations man at the time. That was where I learned my nice manners – as a public relations man.

I told Mike, when we met in New York City, that I had seen his show so long ago. We were nearly the same age, and he was so deep into remembering his youth that he said to me, without any hesitation, 'Schenectady! My God how it snowed!'

He agreed to direct *Happy Birthday, Wanda June*. He was running away from home and some other things – for a little while. So was I. So was Lester.

It is my opinion that the writer and the producer and the director were pleasant, enthusiastic fools about theatre. But Mike assembled a cast, headed by Kevin McCarthy, which was the equal of any cast in New York. Eliot Norton, the Boston critic, told me in conversation that our actors worked together as excitingly as Englishmen. High praise! I said of them, towards the end. 'They're like the The Harlem Globetrotters! Look at 'em go!'

The main trouble was with the author, who didn't really know what he was doing – except running away from home. There I was: all alone in a tiny penthouse borrowed from a friend, six doors down and fifteen floors up from the Theatre de Lys, where the actors were rehearsing. I was writing new beginnings and middles and ends. My nice manners and neat appearance decayed. I came to resemble a madman who was attempting to extract moonbeams from excrement.

We opened on October 7th, 1970, at the de Lys. The reviews were mixed, as they say. We had actors, but no play – or, worse, we had an awfully long, old-fashioned play with no ending. We kept running, though.

And I kept rewriting. I became pathologically suggestible. If somebody had told me to paint my feet blue for the sake of the play, I would have done it solemnly. Blue-footed, I would have asked Lester to do what I was always asking him, 'All right – we're ready. Invite Clive Barnes and John Simon to have another look.' I would do anything anybody told me to do – but go home.

I now thank heaven that my main advisers were the actors, my new family. Their advice, particularly Kevin McCarthy's advice, was expert and beautiful. I was still rewriting six weeks after we opened. And along came an off-Broadway actors' strike.

So we tottered uptown to the Edison Theatre, and opened again. We closed there on March 14th, 1971, after one hundred and forty-two performances. There was standing room only at the final performance, a Sunday matinée. Some good soul shouted, 'Bravo!' The actors had saved the play.

Things die. All things die. My new family dissolved into the late afternoon. As we went our separate ways out of the theatre district, blue movies and peepshows offered to confirm our new solitude, if we cared to drop in.

Walking home along Forty-seventh Street, I remembered having asked Kevin and Nick Coster and Marsha Mason what the end would be like. This was during supper at Duff's, shortly after rehearsals had begun. 'Does being in a play with a person often make that person a friend for life?' I said.

'You'd think it would – and I always think it will,' said Nick.

'When a play closes,' said Marsha, 'everybody promises everybody else that they will go on seeing a lot of each other . . .' She paused to remember the closings she had endured.

Kevin finished the thought for her brusquely, unsentimentally, in the manner of Ernest Hemingway. 'But they *don't*,' he said. He took an iron-jawed bite of hot bread with garlic butter. The subject was closed.

HAPPY BIRTHDAY, WANDA JUNE

CHARACTERS

PENELOPE RYAN, 30
PAUL RYAN, 12, her son
HAROLD RYAN, 55, her husband
COLONEL LOOSELEAF HARPER, 50,
her husband's sidekick
HERB SHUTTLE, 35, a suitor
DR NORBERT WOODLY, 35, a suitor
WANDA JUNE, 10, a ghost
MAJOR SIEGFRIED VON KONIGSWALD, 50
a German ghost
MILDRED, 45, Harold's former wife, a ghost

ACT ONE

SCENE ONE

Silence. Pitch blackness. Animal eyes begin to glow in the darkness. Sounds of the jungle climax in animals fighting. A singer is heard singing the first bars of 'All God's Chillun Got Shoes', HAROLD, LOOSELEAF, PENELOPE *and* WOODLY *stand in a row in the darkness, facing the audience. They are motionless. A city skyline in the early evening materializes outside the windows.*

The lights come up on the living-room of a rich man's apartment, which is densely furnished with trophies of hunts and wars. There is a front door, a door to the master bedroom suite, and a corridor leading to other bedrooms, the kitchen and so on.

PENELOPE. How do you do. My name is Penelope Ryan. This is a simple-minded play about men who enjoy killing – and those who don't.

HAROLD. I am Harold Ryan, her husband, I have killed perhaps two hundred men in wars of various sorts – as a professional soldier. I have killed thousands of other animals as well – for sport.

WOODLY. I am Dr Norbert Woodly – a physician, a healer. I find it disgusting and frightening that a killer should still be a respected member of society. Gentleness must replace violence everywhere, or we are doomed.

PENELOPE. (*to* LOOSELEAF). Would you like to say something about killing, Colonel?

LOOSELEAF (*embarrassed*). Jesus – I dunno. You know. What the heck. Who knows?

PENELOPE. Colonel Harper, retired now, dropped an atom bomb on Nagasaki during the Second World War, killing seventy-four thousand people in a flash.

LOOSELEAF. I dunno, boy.

PENELOPE. You don't *know*?

LOOSELEAF. It was a bitch.

PENELOPE. Thank you. (*To all*) You can leave now. We'll begin.

WOODLY (*to the audience, making a peace sign*). Peace!

(*All but* PENELOPE *exit.*)

PENELOPE (*to the audience*). This is a tragedy. When it's done, my face will be as white as the snows of Kilimanjaro.

(*Hyena laughs.*)

My husband, who kills so much, has been missing for eight years. He disappeared in a light plane over the Amazon Rain Forest, where he hoped to find diamonds as big as cantaloups. His pilot was Colonel Looseleaf Harper, who dropped the bomb on Nagasaki.

(*Hyena laughs.*)

I should explain the doorbells in this apartment. They were built by Abercrombie and Fitch. They are actual recordings of animal cries. The back doorbell is a hyena, which you've just heard. The front doorbell is a lion's roar. (*To the wings*) Would you let them hear it please?

(*Lion roars.*)

Thank you.

(PAUL, *her twelve-year-old son, enters from corridor, a sensitive, neatly dressed little rich boy.*)

And this is my son, Paul. He was only four years old when his father disappeared.

PAUL (*radiantly, sappily*). He's coming back, Mom! He's the bravest, most wonderful man who ever lived.

PENELOPE (*to audience*). I told you this was a simple-minded play.

PAUL. Maybe he'll come back tonight! It's his birthday.

PENELOPE. I know.

PAUL. Stay home tonight!

PENELOPE (*ruefully, for they have been over this before*). Oh, Paul –

PAUL. You're married! You've already got a husband!

PENELOPE. He's a ghost!

PAUL. He's alive!

PENELOPE. Not even Mutual of Omaha thinks so any more.

PAUL. If you have to go out with some guy – can't he be more like Dad? (*Sick*) Herb Shuttle and Norbert Woodly – can't you do better than those two freaks?

PENELOPE (*resentfully*). Thank you, kind sir.

PAUL. A vacuum cleaner salesman and a fairy doctor.

PENELOPE. A *what* kind of doctor?

PAUL. A fairy – a queer. Everybody in the building knows he's a queer.

PENELOPE (*knowing better*). That's an interesting piece of news.

PAUL. You're the only woman he ever took out.

PENELOPE. Not true.

PAUL. Still lives with his mother.

PENELOPE. You know she has no *feet*! You want him to abandon his mother, who has no husband, who has no money of her own, who has no feet?

PAUL. How did she lose her feet?

PENELOPE. In a railroad accident many years ago.

PAUL. I was afraid to ask.

PENELOPE. Norbert was just beginning practice. A real man would have sold her to a catfood company, I suppose. As far as that goes, J. Edgar Hoover still lives with his mother.

PAUL. I didn't know that.

PENELOPE. A lot of people don't.

PAUL. J. Edgar Hoover plays sports.

PENELOPE. I don't really know.

PAUL. The only exercise Dr Woodly ever gets is playing the violin and making that stupid peace sign. (*He makes the peace sign and says the word effeminately.*) Peace, Peace. Peace, everybody.

(*Lion doorbell roars.*)

PENELOPE (*cringing*). I hate that thing.

PAUL. It's beautiful.

(*He goes to door, admits* WOODLY, *whom he loathes openly.*)

WOODLY (*wearing street clothes, carrying a rolled-up poster under his arm*). Peace, everybody – Paul, Penelope.

PAUL. You're taking Mom out tonight?

WOODLY (*to* PENELOPE). You're going out?

PENELOPE. Herb Shuttle is taking me to a fight.

WOODLY. Take plenty of cigars.

PENELOPE. (*An apology, secret from* PAUL) We made the date three months ago.

WOODLY. I must take you to an emergency ward sometime – on a Saturday night. That's also fun. I came to see Selma, as a matter of fact.

PENELOPE. She quit this afternoon.

PAUL. We don't have a maid any more.

WOODLY. Oh?

PENELOPE. The animals made her sneeze and cry too much.

WOODLY. I'm glad somebody finally cried. Every time I come in here and see all this unnecessary death, *I* want to cry. (*Winking at* PAUL, *acknowledging* PAUL's *low opinion of him*) I don't cry, of course. Not manly, you know. Did she try antihistamines?

PENELOPE. They made her so sleepy she couldn't work.

WOODLY. Throw out all this junk. Burn it! This room crawls with tropical disease.

PAUL. Everything stays as it is!

WOODLY. A monument to a man who thought that what the world needed most was more rhinoceros meat.

PAUL (*hotly*). My father!

WOODLY. I apologize. But you didn't know him, and neither did I. How's your asthma?

PAUL. Don't worry about it.

WOODLY. How's the fungus around your thumbnail?

PAUL (*concealing the thumb*). It's fine!

WOODLY. It's jungle rot! This room is making everybody sick! This is your family doctor speaking now. (*Unrolling the poster*) Here – I brought you something else to hang on your wall, for the sake of variety.

PENELOPE (*reading*). 'War is not healthy for children and other living things.' How lovely.

WOODLY. No doubt Paul thinks it stinks.

(*Lion doorbell roars.*)

I hate that thing.

PAUL (*going to the door*). Keeps fairies away!

(*He admits* HERB SHUTTLE, *who carries an Electrolux vacuum cleaner.*)

SHUTTLE (*to* PAUL *affectionately, touching him*). Hi, kid. (*Seeing* WOODLY) Would you look what the cat dragged in.

WOODLY. I'm glad you brought your vacuum cleaner.

SHUTTLE. Is that a fact?

WOODLY. The maid just quit. The place is a mess. You can start in the master bedroom.

PENELOPE. Please –

SHUTTLE. He's not anybody to tell somebody else what to do in a master bedroom.

PENELOPE. I'll get ready, Herb. I didn't expect you this

soon. (*To all*) Please – won't everybody be nice to everybody else while I'm gone?

(*All freeze, except* PENELOPE, *who comes forward to address the audience. Lights on set fade as spotlight comes on.*)

Most men shunned me – even when I nearly swooned for want of love. I might as well have been girdled in a chastity belt. My chastity belt was not made of iron and chains and chickenwire, but of Harold's lethal reputation.

(SHUTTLE *comes into the spotlight.*)

SHUTTLE. I keep having this nightmare – that he catches us.

PENELOPE. Doing what?

SHUTTLE. He'd kill me. He'd be right to kill me, too – the kind of guy he is.

PENELOPE. Or was. We haven't done anything wrong, you know.

SHUTTLE. He'd assume we had.

PENELOPE. That's something, I suppose.

SHUTTLE. All through the day I'm so confident. That's why I'm such a good salesman, you know? I have confidence, and I look like I have confidence, and that gives other people confidence. People laugh sometimes when they find out I'm a vacuum cleaner salesman. They stop laughing, though, when they find out I made forty-three thousand dollars last year. I've got six other salesmen working under me, and what they all plug into is *my* confidence. That's what charges them up.

PENELOPE. I'm glad.

SHUTTLE. I was captain of the wrestling team at Lehigh University.

PENELOPE. I know.

SHUTTLE. If you want to wrestle, you go to Lehigh.

If you want to play tennis, you go to Vanderbilt.

PENELOPE. I don't want to go to Vanderbilt.

SHUTTLE. You don't wrestle if you don't have supreme confidence, and I wrestled. But when I get with you, and I say to myself, 'My God – here I am with the wife of Harold Ryan, one of the great heroes of all time – '

(*Pause.*)

PENELOPE. Yes?

SHUTTLE. Something happens to my confidence.

PENELOPE (*to the audience*). This conversation took place, incidentally, about three months before Harold was declared legally dead.

SHUTTLE. When Harold is definitely out of the picture, Penelope, when I don't have to worry about doing him wrong or you wrong or Paul wrong, I'm going to ask you to be my wife.

PENELOPE. I'm touched.

SHUTTLE. That's when I'll get my confidence back.

PENELOPE. I see.

SHUTTLE. If you'll pardon the expression, that's when you'll see the fur and feathers fly. Good night.

PENELOPE. Good night.

(*Blackout.*)

SCENE TWO

SHUTTLE *and* WOODLY *argue in pitch darkness, with* PAUL *listening and lights come up gradually to full on the living-room the same evening.*

SHUTTLE. You've got to fight from time to time.

WOODLY. Not true.

SHUTTLE. Or get eaten alive.

WOODLY. That's not true either – or needn't be, unless we make it true.

SHUTTLE. Phooey.

WOODLY. Which we do. But we can stop doing that.
> (*The lights are full.* SHUTTLE *and* WOODLY *are bored with each other.* WOODLY *looks out of the window, speaks to an imaginary listener who has more brains than* SHUTTLE. PAUL *hates them both, but prefers* SHUTTLE's *noisy manliness.*)

We simply stop doing that -- dropping things on each other, eating each other alive.

SHUTTLE (*calling*). Penelope! We're late!

PENELOPE (*off, in master bedroom suite*). Coming.

SHUTTLE (*to* PAUL). Women are always late. You'll find out.

WOODLY (*thoughtfully*). The late Mrs Harold Ryan.

SHUTTLE. I'm sick of this argument. I just have one more thing to say: If you elect a President, you support him, no matter what he does. That's the only way you can have a country!

WOODLY. It's the planet that's in ghastly trouble now and all our brothers and sisters thereon.

SHUTTLE. None of my relatives are Chinese Communists. Speak for yourself.

WOODLY. Chinese maniacs and Russian maniacs and American maniacs and French maniacs and British maniacs have turned this lovely, moist, nourishing blue-green ball into a doomsday device. Let a radar set and a computer mistake a hawk or a meteor for a missile, and that's the end of mankind.

SHUTTLE. You can believe that if you want. I talk to guys like you, and I want to commit suicide. (*To* PAUL) You get that weight-lifting set I sent you?

PAUL. It came yesterday. I haven't opened it yet.

WOODLY (*musingly, attempting to find the idea acceptable, even funny, in a way*). Maybe it's supposed to end now. Maybe God wouldn't have it any other way.

SHUTTLE (*to* PAUL). Start with the smallest weights. Every week add a pound or two.

WOODLY. Maybe God has let everybody who ever lived be reborn – so he or she can see how it ends. Even Pithecanthropus erectus and Australopithecus and Sinanthropus pekensis and the Neanderthalers are back on Earth – to see how it ends. They're all on Times Square – making change for peepshows. Or recruiting Marines.

SHUTTLE (*to* PAUL). You ever hear the story about the boy who carried a calf around the barn every day?

WOODLY. He died of a massive rupture.

SHUTTLE. You think you're so funny. You're not even funny. (*To* PAUL) Right? Right? You don't hurt yourself if you start out slow.

WOODLY. You're preparing him for a career in the slaughterhouses of Dubuque? (*To* PAUL) Take care of your body, yes! But don't become a bender of horseshoes and railroad spikes. Don't become obsessed by your musculature. Any one of these poor, dead animals here was a thousand times the athlete you can ever hope to be. Their magic was in their muscles. Your magic is in your brains!

(PENELOPE *enters from the bedroom, dressed for the fight. She wears barbaric jewellery* HAROLD *gave her years ago, a jaguar-skin coat over her shoulders*.)

PENELOPE (*brightly*). Gentlemen! Is this right for a fight? It's been so long.

SHUTTLE. Beautiful! I've never seen that coat.

PENELOPE. Seven jaguars' skins, I'm told. Harold shot every one. Shall we go?

WOODLY (*sick about the slain jaguars*). Oh no! Wear a coat of cotton – wear a coat of wool.

PENELOPE. What?

WOODLY. Wear a coat of domestic mink. For the love of God, though, Penelope, don't lightheartedly advertise that the last of the jaguars died for you.

SHUTTLE. She's my date tonight. What do you want her to do – bring the poor old jaguars back to life with a bicycle pump? Bugger off! Ask Paul what *he* thinks. (*To* PAUL) Your mother looks beautiful – right?

(PAUL *pointedly declines to answer*.)

Kid?

(PAUL *walks away from him*.)

Doesn't your mother look nice?

(*He goes to* PAUL, *wondering what is wrong*.)

Paul?

PAUL (*smoulderingly*). I don't care what she wears.

SHUTTLE. Something's made you sore.

PAUL. Don't worry about it.

SHUTTLE. You bet I'll worry about it. I said something wrong?

PAUL (*close to angry tears*). It's my father's birthday – that's all. (*Facing everybody, raising his voice*) That's all. Who cares about that?

SHUTTLE (*horrified, raising his hand to swear an oath*). I had not the slightest inkling. (*To* PENELOPE, *feeling betrayed*) Why didn't you say so?

PAUL (*bitterly*). She doesn't care! She's not married any more! She's going to have fun! (*To* PENELOPE) I hope you have so much fun you can hardly stand it. (*To* WOODLY) Dr Woodly – I hope you make up even better jokes about my father than the ones you've said so far.

SHUTTLE (*reaching out for* PAUL). Kid – kid –

PAUL (*to* SHUTTLE). And I wish you'd quit touching me all the time. It drives me nuts!

SHUTTLE (*reaching out again*). What's this?

PAUL (*recoiling*). Don't!

SHUTTLE (*aghast*). You sure misunderstood something – and we'd better get it straight.

PAUL. Explain it to them. I'm bugging out of here.
(*He grabs a jacket from the chair.* SHUTTLE *is in his way.*)
Don't touch me. Get out of the way.

SHUTTLE. Men can touch other men, and it doesn't mean a thing. Haven't you ever seen football players after they've won the Superbowl?

PENELOPE (*to* PAUL). Where will you be?

PAUL. Anywhere but here. I'd just sit here and cry about the way my father's been forgotten.

SHUTTLE. I *worship* your father. That stuffed alligator your mother gave me – the one he shot? It's the proudest thing in my apartment.

PAUL (*at the door*). Everybody talks about how rotten kids act. Grown-ups can be pretty rotten, too. (*He exits through front door, slams it.*)

SHUTTLE (*heartbroken*). Kid – kid –

WOODLY. It's good. Let him go.

SHUTTLE. If he'd just come out for the Little League,

the way I asked him, he'd find out we touch all the time – shove each other, slug each other, and just horse around. I'm going to go get him –

WOODLY. Don't! Let him have all the privacy he wants. Let him grieve, let him rage. There has never been a funeral for his father.

PENELOPE. I never knew when to hold it – or who to ask, or what to say.

WOODLY. Tonight's the night.

SHUTTLE. If he'd just get into scouting, and camp out some, and see how everybody rough-houses around the fire –

WOODLY. What a beautiful demonstration this is of the utter necessity of rites of passage.

SHUTTLE. I feel like I've been double-crossed. (*To* PENELOPE, *peevishly*) If you'd just told me it was Harold's birthday –

PENELOPE. What then?

SHUTTLE. We could have had some kind of birthday party for him. We could have taken Paul to the fight with us.

WOODLY. Minors aren't allowed at fights.

SHUTTLE. Then we'd stay home and eat venison or something, and look through the scrapbooks. I've got a friend who has a whole freezer full of striped bass and caribou meat. (*Going to the front door*) I'm going to bring that boy back. (*He exits through front door.*)

WOODLY (*going to* PENELOPE). This is very good for us.

PENELOPE. It is?

WOODLY. The wilder Paul is tonight, the calmer he'll be tomorrow.

PENELOPE. As long as he keeps out of the park.

WOODLY. After this explosion, I think, he'll be able to accept the fact that his mother is going to marry again.

PENELOPE. The only thing I ever told him about life was, 'Keep out of the park after the sun goes down.'

WOODLY. We've got to dump Shuttle. (*Pointing to the vacuum cleaner*) He brings his vacuum cleaner on dates?

PENELOPE. That's the XKE.

WOODLY. The what?

PENELOPE. It's an experimental model. He doesn't dare leave it in his car, for fear it will fall into the hands of competition.

WOODLY. What kind of a life is that?

PENELOPE. He told me one time what the proudest moment of his life was. He made Eagle Scout when he was twenty-nine years old. (*Clinging to him suddenly*) Oh, Norbert – promise me that Paul has not gone into the park!

WOODLY (*pause*). If you warned him against it as much as you say, it's almost a certainty.

PENELOPE (*petrified*). No! Oh no! Three people murdered in there in the last six weeks! The police won't even go in there any more.

WOODLY. I wish Paul luck.

PENELOPE. It's suicide!

WOODLY. I'd be dead by now if that were the case.

PENELOPE. Meaning?

WOODLY. Every night, Penelope, for the past two years, I've made it a point to walk through the park at midnight.

PENELOPE. Why would you do that?

WOODLY. To show myself how brave I am. The issue's in doubt, you know – since I'm always for peace –

PENELOPE. I'm amazed.

WOODLY. Me, too. I know something not even the police know – what's in the park at midnight. Nothing. Or, when I'm in there, there's me in there. Fear and nobody and me.

PENELOPE. And maybe Paul. What about the murderers? They're in there!

WOODLY. They didn't murder me.

PENELOPE. Paul's only twelve years old.

WOODLY. He can make the sound of human footsteps – which is a terrifying sound.

PENELOPE. We've got to rescue him.

WOODLY. If he is in the park, luck is all that can save him now, and there's plenty of that.

PENELOPE. He's not your son.

WOODLY. No. But he's going to be. If he is in the park and he comes out safely on the other side, I can say to him, 'You and I are the only men with balls enough to walk through the park at midnight.' (*Pause.*) On that we can build.

PENELOPE. It's a jungle out there.

WOODLY. That's been said before.

PENELOPE. He'd go to a movie. I think that's what he'd do. If I were sure he was in a movie, I could stop worrying. We could have him paged.

(*Lion doorbell roars.*)

WOODLY. I hate that thing.

(*He opens door, admits* SHUTTLE, *who carries a bakery box.*)

PENELOPE. Did you see him?

SHUTTLE. Yeah.

PENELOPE. Is he all right?

SHUTTLE. Far as I know.

PENELOPE. Is he coming home?

SHUTTLE. He ditched me. He started running, and I started running, then he lost me in the park.

PENELOPE. The park!

SHUTTLE. It's dark in there.

PENELOPE. And that's where he is!

SHUTTLE. I figure he ducked in one place and ducked out another.

PENELOPE (*disgusted with him*). You figure!

SHUTTLE. Then I saw this bakery store that was still open, so I bought a birthday cake.

PENELOPE. A what?

SHUTTLE. For Harold. When Paul comes home, we can have some birthday cake.

PENELOPE. How nice.

SHUTTLE. They had this cake somebody else hadn't picked up. It says, 'Happy Birthday, Somebody Else.'

WOODLY. 'Happy Birthday, Wanda June!'

SHUTTLE. We can take off the 'Wanda June' with a butter knife.

PENELOPE. Did you talk to Paul?

SHUTTLE. Before he started to run. He said his father carried a key to this apartment around his neck – and someday we'd all hear the sound of that key in the door.

PENELOPE. We've got to find him. (*Preparing to exit through front door*) I want you to show me exactly where you saw him last. (*To* WOODLY) And you stay here, Norbert in case he comes home. (*To* SHUTTLE) That's all he said – the thing about the key?

SHUTTLE. He said one other thing. It wasn't very nice.

PENELOPE. What was it?

SHUTTLE. He told me to take a flying fuck at the moon. (*Blackout.*)

SCENE THREE

Darkness. Lights come up on living-room. WOODLY *is alone, asleep on the couch.*

HAROLD *lets himself and* LOOSELEAF *in through the front door – quietly.* HAROLD *has a full beard and a paunch.* LOOSELEAF *is skinnier. He has a handlebar moustache. Both wear new sports clothes and smoke expensive cigars.* HAROLD *is calm.* LOOSELEAF *is nervous, confused. They prowl the room cautiously, checking this and that.* HAROLD *awakens* WOODLY *by playing with his feet.*

WOODLY (*startled*). Ooops.

HAROLD (*to* LOOSELEAF, *very amused*). Ooops.

WOODLY. Can I – uh – help you gentlemen?

HAROLD (*moving downstage, feeling at home*). Gentlemen – that's nice.

WOODLY (*to* LOOSELEAF). You startled me.

LOOSELEAF. Yeah. We just got here.

WOODLY. I thought you might be burglars – but you're not, I hope.

LOOSELEAF. Nope. (*Idiotically, incapable of deception*) I got a lot of stuff.

WOODLY (*looking at him closely*). You do?

HAROLD. The door was unlocked. Is it always unlocked?

WOODLY. It's always *locked*.

HAROLD. But here *you* are inside, aren't you?

WOODLY. You're – you're old friends of Harold Ryan?

HAROLD. We tried to be. We tried to be.

WOODLY. He's dead, you know.

HAROLD. Dead! Such a *final* word. Dead! (*To* LOOSE-
LEAF) Did you hear that?

LOOSELEAF. Yup.

> (*Telephone rings.* WOODLY *answers, keeping his eyes
> on the bizarre guests.*)

WOODLY. Hello? Oh – hello, Mother.

HAROLD (*to* LOOSELEAF). Hello, Mother.

WOODLY. . . . Who? . . . Did she say how far apart the
pains were? . . . When was that? . . . Oh dear.

HAROLD. Oh dear.

WOODLY. Call her back – tell her to head for the
hospital. Tell the hospital to expect her. I'll leave right
now. (*He hangs up, faces the intruders.*) Look – I'm
sorry – I have to go.

HAROLD. We'll miss you so.

WOODLY. Look – this isn't my apartment, and there
isn't anybody else here. Mrs Ryan won't be home for
a while.

HAROLD. Oh, oh, oh – I thought it *was* your apartment.
You seemed so at home here.

WOODLY. I'm a neighbour. I have the apartment across
the hall. I have to go to the hospital now. An *emergency.*

> (HAROLD *is unstirred.*)

I mean – I can't leave you here. You'll have to go. I'll
tell Mrs Ryan you were here. You can come back later.

HAROLD. Ahh – then she's still alive.

WOODLY. She's fine. Please –

HAROLD. And still Mrs Harold Ryan?

WOODLY. Will you please go? An emergency!

HAROLD. She still has just the one child – the boy?

> (*He moves slowly towards the front door, with*
> WOODLY *trying to hustle him and* LOOSELEAF *out.*)

WOODLY. Yes! Yes! The boy! One boy!

HAROLD (*stopping*). And what, exactly, is your relation-
ship to Mrs Ryan?

WOODLY. Neighbour! Doctor! I live across the hall.

HAROLD. And you come into Mrs Ryan's apartment as often as you please, looking into various health matters?

WOODLY. Yes! Please! You've got to get out right now! (HAROLD *moves a little more, stops again.*)

HAROLD. Just her neighbour and doctor? That's all?

WOODLY (*at the end of his patience, blurting*). And her fiancé!

HAROLD (*delighted*). And her fiancé! How nice. I hope you'll be very happy – or is that what one says to the woman?

WOODLY. I've got to run! (*He turns out the overhead light.*)

HAROLD. You wish the woman good luck, and you tell the man how fortunate he is. That's how it goes.

WOODLY (*holding open the front door*). I've literally got to run!

HAROLD. I won't try to keep up with you. I'm not as fast on my feet as I once was.

(*All three exit. A moment later,* HAROLD *lets himself and* LOOSELEAF *in again with a key. He turns on the light again, roams the room, reacquainting himself with his beloved trophies.* LOOSELEAF *is jangled by the adventure.* HAROLD *chucks a lioness under her chin.*)

Miss me, baby?

LOOSELEAF. I dunno, boy.

HAROLD. Hm?

LOOSELEAF. It's a bitch.

HAROLD (*quietly*). A bitch.

LOOSELEAF. Didn't recognize you.

HAROLD. We've never met.

LOOSELEAF. I wonder who'll recognize us first? They'll wet their pants.

HAROLD. I hope the men do. I would rather the women didn't.

LOOSELEAF. I'm gonna wet *my* pants. (*He laughs idiotically.*)

HAROLD (*looking around himself*). Home, sweet home.

LOOSELEAF. One thing, anyway – at least Penelope didn't throw out all your crap. I bet Alice threw out all my crap after I'd been gone a week.

HAROLD. We'll see.

(HAROLD, *who wants to savour the early moments of his homecoming alone, now tries to get the very jumpy* LOOSELEAF *out of the apartment.*)

It appears that we're going to have to wait awhile for any more action here, Colonel. Why don't you run on home while the evening's young.

LOOSELEAF. Home. Jesus. (*He makes his hands tremble.*) I'm like *this*. Home!

HAROLD. Home is important to a man.

LOOSELEAF. You know what gets me?

HAROLD (*absently*). No.

LOOSELEAF. How all the magazines show tits today.

HAROLD. Um.

LOOSELEAF. Used to be against the law, didn't it?

HAROLD (*fed up with* LOOSELEAF). I suppose.

LOOSELEAF (*making no move to leave*). Must have changed that law.

(*Silence, while* HAROLD *attempts to be alone, even though* LOOSELEAF *is still present.*)

HAROLD (*thoughtfully hefting a broadsword, admiring its balance and strength*). Home.

LOOSELEAF. You know what gets me?

(HAROLD *does not respond.*)

You know what gets me?

HAROLD (*to himself*). Oh, shit.

LOOSELEAF (*finding enough encouragement in this*). How

everybody says 'fuck' and 'shit' all the time. I used to be scared shitless I'd say 'fuck' or 'shit' in public, by accident. Now everybody says 'fuck' and 'shit', 'fuck' and 'shit' all the time. Something very big must have happened while we were out of the country.

HAROLD (*flatly*). Looseleaf – will you get the hell home?

LOOSELEAF. At least we found the diamonds.

HAROLD. At least!

LOOSELEAF. I'd really feel stupid if we didn't bring anything back home.

HAROLD. It's enough that you've brought yourself home!

LOOSELEAF. I wish you'd tell Alice that. And that goddam Mrs Wheeler.

HAROLD (*hotly*). Tell them yourself!

LOOSELEAF. You don't know my mother-in-law, boy.

HAROLD. After eight years in the jungle with you, I know Mrs Wheeler better than I know anybody in the universe!

LOOSELEAF. I didn't tell you everything.

HAROLD. The time we were in a tree for fourteen days, you certainly *tried* to tell me everything about Mrs Wheeler.

LOOSELEAF. I didn't even scratch the surface. You're lucky, boy. You come home, and nobody's here. When I go home, *everybody's* going to be there.

HAROLD. This room is full of ghosts.

LOOSELEAF. You're lucky, boy. My house is gonna be filled with *people*.

(HAROLD *ignores this, attempts to savour the ghosts in the room.*)

You know what gets me?

HAROLD. Go home!

LOOSELEAF. Thank God we found the fucking diamonds!

HAROLD. The hell with the diamonds!

LOOSELEAF. You were rich *before*. This is the first time I was ever rich.

HAROLD. Go home! Show them how rich you are for a change!

LOOSELEAF. Can I have the Cadillac?

HAROLD. Take the Cadillac and drive it off a cliff, for all I care.

LOOSELEAF. What'll you do for transportation?

HAROLD. I'll buy a hundred more Cadillacs. Go home!

LOOSELEAF. You know what gets me about that Cadillac?

HAROLD. Go home!

LOOSELEAF. When I drive it, I feel like I'm in the middle of a great big wad of bubblegum. I don't hear anything. I don't feel anything. I figure somebody else is driving. It's a bitch.

HAROLD. Go home.

LOOSELEAF. I'm liable to find anything!

HAROLD. That's the point! Walk in there and find whatever there *is* to find – before Alice can cover it up.

LOOSELEAF. I know, I know. I dunno. At least she's in the same house. Sure was spooky, looking in the window there, and there she was.

HAROLD. So long, Colonel.

LOOSELEAF. You know what gets me?

HAROLD (*taking hold of* LOOSELEAF *and steering him to the front door*). Let's talk about it some other time.

LOOSELEAF. How short the skirts are.

HAROLD (*opening the door*). Good night, Colonel. It's been beautiful.

LOOSELEAF. Something very important about sex must have happened while we were gone.

(HAROLD *shoves him out of the apartment and shuts the door.* HAROLD *starts to roam the room again, but the lion doorbell roars.*)

HAROLD (*going to the door*). Hell!

(HAROLD *opens the door*. LOOSELEAF *comes in.*)

LOOSELEAF. You know what gets me? Those guys who went to the moon! To the *moon*, boy!

HAROLD. Leave me alone! After eight years of horrendously close association, the time has come to part! I crave solitude and time for reflection – and then a reunion in privacy with my own flesh and blood. You and I may not meet again for months!

LOOSELEAF. Months?

HAROLD. I'm certainly not going to come horning back into your life tomorrow, and I will not welcome your horning back into mine. A chapter has ended. We are old comrades – at a parting of the ways.

LOOSELEAF (*bleakly, shrugging*). I'm lonesome already. (*He exits.*)

HAROLD (*roaming the room again*). The moon. The new heroism – put a village idiot into a pressure cooker, seal it up tight, and shoot him at the moon. (*To his portrait*) Hello there, young man. In case you're wondering, I could beat the shit out of you. And any woman choosing between us – sorry, kid, she'd choose me. (*Pleased with the room*) I must say, this room is very much as I left it. (*He sees the cake.*) What's this? A cake? 'Happy Birthday, Wanda June'? Who the hell is Wanda June?

(*Blackout.*)

SCENE FOUR

Music indicates happiness, innocence, and weightlessness. Spotlight comes up on WANDA JUNE, *a lisping eight-year-old in a starched party dress. She is as cute as Shirley Temple.*

WANDA JUNE. Hello, I am Wanda June. Today was going to be my birthday, but I was hit by an ice-cream truck before I could have my party. I am dead now. I am in Heaven. That is why my parents did not pick up the cake at the bakery. I am not mad at the ice-cream truck driver, even though he was drunk when he hit me. It didn't hurt much. It wasn't even as bad as the sting of a bumblebee. I am really *happy* here! It's so much fun. I am glad the driver was drunk. If he hadn't been, I might not have got to Heaven for years and years and years. I would have had to go to high school first, and then beauty college. I would have had to get married and have babies and everything. Now I can just play and play and play. Any time I want any pink cotton candy I can have some. Everybody up here is happy – the animals and the dead soldiers and people who went to the electric chair and everything. They're all glad for whatever sent them here. Nobody is mad. We're all too busy playing shuffleboard. So if you think of killing somebody, don't worry about it. Just go ahead and do it. Whoever you do it to should kiss you for doing it. The soldiers up here just love the shrapnel and the tanks and the bayonets and the dum dums that let them play shuffleboard all the time – and drink beer.

(*Spotlight begins to dim and carnival music on a steam calliope begins to intrude, until, at the end of the speech,* WANDA JUNE *is drowned out and the stage is black.*)

We have merry-go-rounds that don't cost anything to ride on. We have Ferris wheels. We have Little League and girls' basketball. There's a drum and bugle corps anybody can join. For people who like golf, there is a par-three golf course and a driving range, with never any waiting. If you just want to sit and loaf, why that's all right, too. Gourmet specialities are cooked to your order and served at any time of night or day . . .

(*Sudden silence.*)

WOODY WOODPECKER VOICE. Ha ha ha *ha* ha!

(*Pistol shot.*)

You got me, pal.

(*Silence.*

Spotlight comes up on LOOSELEAF HARPER, *who wears the clothes he will wear in the next scene – new sports clothes, a shirt open at the neck. As always, he is friendly and embarrassed.*)

LOOSELEAF. When Penelope asked me to say something about dropping the bomb on Nagasaki, I didn't give a very good answer. I guess. It's a very complicated question. Jesus – you *know*? You have to explain what it's like to be in the Air Force and how they give you your orders and all that. What it feels like to be in a plane, what the world looks like down there. After I got home from the war, the minister of my church asked me if I would speak to a scout troop that met in the church basement. So I did. They met on Thursday nights. I used to belong to that troop. I never made Eagle Scout. But you know something? It's a very strange kind of kid that makes Eagle Scout. They always seem so lonesome, like they'd worked real hard to get a job nobody else cares about. They get a whole bunch of merit badges. That's how you get to be an Eagle Scout. I don't think I had over five or six merit badges. The only one I remember is Public Health. That was a bitch. The Boy Scout Manual said I was supposed to find out what my town did about sewage. Jesus, they just dumped it all in Sugar Creek.

(*He laughs idiotically.*)

Sugar Creek! That was a long time ago, but it's all coming back to me now. There was another merit badge you could get for roller skating. There used to be a roller rink at a bend in Sugar Creek, up above where the sewage went in. I got in a fight there one time. I had on roller skates, and the guy I was fighting had on basketball shoes. He had a tremendous advantage over me. He was a little guy, but he beat the shit out of me. I had to laugh like hell. Don't ever fight a guy when you've got on roller skates.

(*Silence.*)

Jesus – I remember my mother used to make me chew bananas for a full minute before I swallowed – so I wouldn't get sick. Makes you wonder what else your parents told you that wasn't *true*.

(*Blackout.*)

SCENE FIVE

Spotlight comes up on HAROLD. *He sits on the front seat of an imaginary car. The seat is covered with zebra skin.*

HAROLD. The night I met Penelope, I had no beard – so imagine me, if you can, without a beard. Actually, I wasn't as good-looking then as I am now. And, if anything, my health has improved. At any rate – I had just come home from Kenya – to discover that my third wife, Mildred, like the two before her, had become a drunken bum. In my experience, alcoholism is far more prevalent among women than men. So I got into my automobile –

> (*He pantomimes turning the ignition key. The sound of a starter and a powerful engine responds. He pantomimes putting the car in gear and driving away from the kerb. Appropriate sounds are heard.*)

I drove through the night, until I was attracted by a sign which said –

> (*Spotlight comes up on* PENELOPE, *who wears a skimpy carhop outfit she has had on under her coat in the previous scene.*)

'Hamburger Heaven.'

PENELOPE. Heaven.

> (HAROLD *pantomimes swerving into Hamburger Heaven. Tyres squeal. He pantomimes a stop, kills the engine. He blows his imaginary horn. A real horn blows the bugle call for 'charge'.* PENELOPE *crosses to* HAROLD.)

Can I help you, sir?

HAROLD. I think so, daughter. How old are you?

PENELOPE. Eighteen – (*pause*) and a half.

HAROLD. A springbok, an oryx, a gemsbok – a gazelle.

PENELOPE. Sir?

HAROLD. Raw hamburger, please – and a whole onion. I want to eat the onion like an apple. Do you understand?

PENELOPE. Yes, sir. (*To the audience*) It was a very unusual automobile. It was a Cadillac, but it had water buffalo horns where the bumpers should be. (*To* HAROLD) And what to drink?

HAROLD. What time do you get off work, my child?

PENELOPE. I'm sorry, sir, I'm engaged to be married. My boyfriend would be mad if I went out with another man.

HAROLD. Did you ever daydream that you would one day meet a friendly millionaire?

PENELOPE. I'm engaged.

HAROLD. Daughter – I love you very much.

PENELOPE. You don't even *know* me.

HAROLD. You are woman. I know woman well.

PENELOPE. This is crazy.

HAROLD. Destiny often seems that way. You're going to marry me.

PENELOPE. What do you do for a living?

HAROLD. My parents died in an automobile accident when I was sixteen years old. They left me a brewery and a baseball team – and other things. I *live* for a living. I've just come back from Kenya – in Africa. I've been hunting Mau Mau there.

PENELOPE. Some kind of animal?

HAROLD. The pelt is black. It's a kind of man.

(*Blackout.*)

SCENE SIX

Curtain rises on empty living-room. PAUL *lets himself in with a key.*

PAUL. Mom?
  (*Silence.*)
  Herb?
  (*Silence.*)
  Dr Woodly? (*He advances into room uneasily.*) Hello?
  (*He sees the cake.*) A cake? Who's Wanda June?
    (HAROLD *enters quietly from the kitchen, holding a can of beer.*)
  Anybody home?
HAROLD. As a matter of fact –
PAUL (*nearly jumping out of his skin*). Sir?
HAROLD. As a matter of fact – *I* am home.
PAUL (*thinking* HAROLD *may be a burglar*). Hello.
HAROLD (*simply*). Hello.
PAUL. Are you – (*His voice fails him*).
HAROLD (*hoping to be recognized*). You were about to ask a question?
PAUL. Are you – do you –
HAROLD. Ask it!
PAUL (*blurting*). Do you know who Wanda June is?
HAROLD. Life has denied me that thrill.
PAUL. Do you mind if I ask who you are?
HAROLD. Mind? (*Aside*) God, yes, I mind. (*To* PAUL) I'm your father's friend. A man claiming to be the family physician let me in a while ago.
PAUL. Dr Woodly.

HAROLD. Dr Woodly. I should make a little list.

PAUL. Is anybody besides you here now?

HAROLD. The doctor was called away on an emergency.
I think it was birth.

PAUL. Where's Mom?

HAROLD. You don't *know* where your mother is?
Does she put on a short skirt and go drinking all
night?

PAUL. She went to the fight with Herb Shuttle, I guess.

HAROLD. You think you could find me a pencil and
paper?

PAUL. I'll see. (*He rummages through a drawer.*)

HAROLD. And you've been roaming the streets while
your mother is God-knows-where?

PAUL. I was going to a funny movie, but I changed my
mind. If you're depressed, laughing doesn't help much.
(*He gives* HAROLD *pencil and paper.*)
When did you know my father?

HAROLD. Man and boy.

PAUL. Everybody says he was so brave.

HAROLD. Even this – 'Herb Shuttle', you said?

PAUL. He *worships* Father.

HAROLD (*pleased*). Ah! And what sort of man *is* this
worshipper?

PAUL. He's a vacuum cleaner salesman.

HAROLD (*deflated*). I see. (*Recovering*) And he came into
the apartment one day, to demonstrate his wares, and
your mother, as it happened, was charmingly *en
déshabillé* –

PAUL. She met him at college.

HAROLD (*startled*). College!

PAUL. They were in the same creative writing class.

HAROLD. College?

PAUL. She has a master's degree in English literature.

HAROLD. What a pity! Educating a beautiful woman is

like pouring honey into a fine Swiss watch. Everything stops.

(*Pause.*)

And the doctor? He worships your father, too?

PAUL. He insults him all the time.

HAROLD (*delighted*). Excellent!

PAUL. What's good about that?

HAROLD. It makes life spicy.

PAUL. He doesn't do it in front of me, but he does it with Mother. (*Indicating* HAROLD'*s portrait*) You know what he called Father one time?

HAROLD. No.

PAUL. 'Harold, the Patron Saint of Taxidermy.'

HAROLD (*measuring his opponent*). What does he do – of an athletic nature?

PAUL. Nothing. He plays a violin in a doctors' quartet.

HAROLD. Aha! He has a brilliant military record, I'm sure.

PAUL. He was a stretcher-bearer in the Korean War.

(*Pause.*)

Were you in a war with Father?

HAROLD. Big ones, little ones, teeny-weeny ones – just and otherwise.

PAUL. Tell me some true stories about Dad.

HAROLD (*unused to the word*). 'Dad'? (*Accepting it*) Dad. (*To himself*) The boy wants tales of derring-do. Name a country.

PAUL. England?

HAROLD (*disgusted*). Oh hell.

PAUL. Dad was never in England?

HAROLD. Behind a desk for a little while. (*Contemptuously*) A desk! They had him planning air raids. A city can't flee like a coward or fight like a man, and the choice between fleeing and fighting was at the core of the life of Harold Ryan. There was only one thing he enjoyed more than watching someone make that choice, and that was making the choice himself. Ask about Spain, where he was the youngest soldier in the Abraham Lincoln Brigade. He was a famous sniper. They called him 'La Picadura' – 'the sting'.

PAUL (*echoing wonderingly*). 'The sting'.

HAROLD. As in 'Death, where is thy sting?' He killed at least fifty men, wounded hundreds more.

PAUL (*slightly dismayed at such murderousness*). 'The sting.'

HAROLD. Ask about the time he and I were parachuted into Yugoslavia to join a guerilla band – in the war against the Nazis.

PAUL. Tell me that.

HAROLD. I saw your father fight Major Siegfried von Konigswald, the Beast of Yugoslavia, hand to hand.

PAUL (*his excitement rising*). Tell me that! Tell me that!

HAROLD. Hid by day – fought by night. At sunset one day, your father and I, peering through field-glasses saw a black Mercedes draw up to a village inn. It was escorted by two motorcyclists and an armoured car. Out of the Mercedes stepped one of the most hateful men in all of history – the Beast of Yugoslavia.

PAUL. Wow.

HAROLD. We blacked our hands and faces. At midnight we crept out of the forest and into the village. The name of the village was Mhravitch. Remember that name!

PAUL. Mhravitch.

HAROLD. We came up behind a sentry, and your father slit his throat before he could utter a sound.

PAUL (*involuntarily*). Uck.

HAROLD. Don't care for cold steel? A knife is worse than a bullet?

PAUL. I don't know.

T–C

HAROLD. The story gets hairier. Should I stop?

PAUL. Go on.

HAROLD. We caught another Kraut alone in a back lane. Your father choked him to death with a length of piano wire. Your father was quite a virtuoso with piano wire. That's nicer than a knife, isn't it – as long as you don't look at the face afterwards. The face turns a curious shade of avocado. I must ask the doctor why that is. At any rate, we stole into the back of the inn, and, with the permission of the management, we poisoned the wine of six Krauts who were carousing there.

PAUL. Where did you get the poison?

HAROLD. We carried cyanide capsules. We were supposed to swallow them in case we were captured. It was your father's opinion that the Krauts needed them more than we did at the time.

PAUL. And one of them was the Beast of Yugoslavia?

HAROLD. The Beast was upstairs, and he came running downstairs for his men were making loud farewells and last wills and testaments – editorializing about the hospitality they had received. And your father said to him in perfect German, which he had learned in the Spanish Civil War. 'Major, something tragic seems to have happened to your bodyguard. I am Harold Ryan, of the United States of America. You, I believe, are the Beast of Yugoslavia.'

(*Blackout.*)

SCENE SEVEN

Silence. Pitch blackness. The sounds of a Nazi rally come up slowly: 'Sieg Heil! Sieg Heil! Sieg Heil!' Spotlight comes up on MAJOR SIEGFRIED VON KONIGSWALD, *an officer in the dreaded SS. He is in full ceremonial uniform. The sounds fade.*

VON KONIGSWALD (*sadly, resignedly, remembering*). Ja ja. Ja ja.

(*Pause.*)

I am Major Siegfried von Konigswald. They used to call me 'The Beast of Yugoslavia', on account of all the people I had tortured and shot – and hanged. We'd bop 'em on the head. We'd hook 'em up to the electricity. We'd stick 'em with hypodermic syringes full of all kinds of stuff. One time we killed a guy with orange juice. There was a train wreck, and two of the freight cars were loaded with oranges, so we had oceans of orange juice. It was a joke – how much orange juice we had. And we were interrogating a guy one day, and he wouldn't talk, and the next thing I know – somebody's filling up this big syringe with orange juice.

(*Pause.*)

There was a guerrilla war going on. You couldn't tell who was a guerrilla and who wasn't. Even if you got one, it was still a civilian you got. Telling Americans what a guerrilla war is like – that's coals to Newcastle. How do you like that for idiomatic English? 'Coals to Newcastle.'

(*He laughs.*)

That Harold Ryan – he says he spoke to me in perfect German? He talks German like my ass chews gum. I'm glad to hear the wonderful thing he said before he killed me. I sure didn't understand it the first time around. I figured he was a Lithuanian or something, which will give you an idea of how wrong you can be. All I knew was he was very proud about something, and he had a machine pistol, and it was aimed at me. The woods were full of all kinds of nuts who were proud of some damn thing or other, and they all had guns. They were always looking for revenge. You find a way to bottle revenge – that's the end of Schnapps *und* Coca-Cola.

(*Pause.*)

Harold Ryan said he killed maybe two hundred guys. I killed a hundred times that many, I bet. That's still peanuts, of course, compared to what that crazy Looseleaf did. Harold and me – we was doing it the hard way. I hope the record books will show that. There should be a little star or something by the names of the guys who did it the hard way.

(*Pause.*)

I'm up in Heaven now, like that little Wanda June kid. I wasn't hit by no ice-cream truck. Harold Ryan killed me with his bare hands. He was good. My eyes popped out. My tongue stuck out like a red banana. I shit in my pants. It was a mess.

(*Pause.*)

When I got up on the day I died, I said, 'What a beautiful day this is. What a beautiful part of the world.' The whole planet was beautiful. Up here I meet guys from other planets.

(*He laughs.*)

We got some really crazy-looking guys up here. Their

planets weren't anywhere near as nice as Earth. They had clouds all the time. They never saw a clear blue sky. They never saw snow. They never saw an ocean. They had some little lakes, but you couldn't go swimming in them. The lakes was acid. You go swimming, you dissolve. We got some guys up here who got shoved in them lakes. They dissolved.

(*Pause.*)

Harold Ryan stopped talking German to me there in Yugoslavia. He switched to English, so I finally got some kind of idea what he was so burned up about. He wanted revenge for the guy we killed with orange juice. I don't know how he ever found out about it. There was just three of us there when we did it – me and two regular military doctors. Somebody who cleaned up afterwards must have squealed. If I'd lived through the war, and they tried me for war crimes and all that, I'd have to tell the court, I guess, 'I was only following orders, as a good soldier should. Hitler *told* me to kill this guy with orange juice.'

(*Blackout.*)

SCENE EIGHT

Darkness. Lights come up on living-room. HAROLD *has just finished telling his true war story to* PAUL.

HAROLD. Mhravitch. Remember that name.

PAUL. Mhravitch.

HAROLD. The name will live forever. It was there that Harold Ryan slew the Beast of Yugoslavia. Mhravitch.

PAUL. When I grow up, I'm going to go to Mhravitch.

HAROLD. It's rather a disappointment these days. It isn't there any more.

PAUL. Sir?

HAROLD. The Germans shot everybody who lived there, then levelled it, ploughed it, planted turnips and cabbages in the fertile ground. They wished revenge for the slaying of the Beast of Yugoslavia. To their twisted way of thinking, your father had butchered an Eagle Scout. (*Abruptly*) Play lots of contact sports?

PAUL. I wanted to go out for football, but Mom was afraid I'd get hurt.

HAROLD. You're *supposed* to get hurt!

PAUL. Dr Woodly says he's seen hundreds of children permanently injured by football. He says that when there's a war, everybody goes but football players.

HAROLD. Does it bother you to have your mother engaged to a man like that?

PAUL. They're not engaged.

HAROLD. *He* seems to think they are. He *told* me they were.

PAUL. Oh, no, no, no, no, no. It can't be. How embarrassing.

HAROLD (*unexpectedly moved*). You're a very good boy to respond that way.

PAUL. No, no, no, no, no.

HAROLD. I'd like to use the sanitary facilities, if I may.

PAUL. Go ahead. (*As* HAROLD *exits*) No, no, no, no.
(PENELOPE *and* SHUTTLE *enter through front door. They are tremendously relieved to see* PAUL.)

PENELOPE. Thank God!

SHUTTLE. What a relief!

PENELOPE (*going to* PAUL). My baby's safe!
(PAUL *angrily avoids her touch*).
What's the matter now?

SHUTTLE. We got a birthday cake, kid. Did you see the cake?

PAUL. Are you and Dr Woodly engaged?

PENELOPE (*stunned*). Who have you been talking to?

PAUL. What difference does that make? Is Dr Woodly going to be my father now?
(*Pause.*)

PENELOPE. Yes, he is.

PAUL (*a stifled, gargling cry*). Aaaaaaaaaaaaaaaaaah!

SHUTTLE (*sick*). That goes double for *me*.

PAUL. I don't want to live any more.

SHUTTLE. I feel like I want to yell my head off – just yell anything. (*Yelling*) Bulllllllllllllllllllllll-dickey!

PAUL. I'll kill myself.

SHUTTLE. The wife of Harold Ryan is going to marry a pansy next? This is the end of Western Civilization as far as I'm concerned. You must be crazy as a fruitcake.

PENELOPE. Possibly.

SHUTTLE. How long has this been going on?

PENELOPE. A week. We were waiting for the right time to –

SHUTTLE. I feel as though I had been made a perfect chump of.

PENELOPE. I'm sorry.

SHUTTLE. Marry me instead.

PENELOPE. Thank you, Herb. You're a wonderful man. You really are. Everybody respects you for what you've done for scouting and the Little League.

SHUTTLE. You're saying no.

PENELOPE. I'm saying no – and thank you.

SHUTTLE. I didn't make my move fast enough. That's it, isn't it? I was too respectful.

PENELOPE. You were wonderful.

SHUTTLE. What's so wonderful if I lost the sale? (*Turning to* PAUL) You poor kid.

PAUL. Don't touch me.

SHUTTLE. Wouldn't you rather have your mother marry me than him?

PAUL. No.

SHUTTLE (*moving dazedly towards the front door*). All my dreams have suddenly collapsed.
   (*Pause.*)
We did have a lot of laughs together, Penelope.

PENELOPE. It's true.

SHUTTLE. Well – it was nice while it lasted. Thanks for the memories.
   (*He exits.*
   Silence. A toilet flushes loudly and complicatedly.)

PENELOPE. Is Norbert still here?

PAUL. No.

PENELOPE. Then who flushed the toilet?

PAUL. Father's friend.

PENELOPE. What's his name?

PAUL. Don't know.

PENELOPE. For heaven sakes!
   (HAROLD *enters, still adjusting his trousers.*)

How do you do?

HAROLD. How *you* do, Mrs Ryan? I'd heard you were beautiful, and so you are. Am I intruding here?

PENELOPE. Not at all.

HAROLD. I couldn't help overhearing that you were about to get married again.

(PENELOPE *has now recognized him, but attempts to protect herself from shock by pretending that she has not.*)

PENELOPE. Our family physician has asked me to marry him. Paul needs the guidance and companionship that only a man can give. He isn't at all like Harold. But then again, I'm not the woman I was eight years ago. (*She slumps into a chair, buries her face in her hands.*)

PAUL. Mom?

PENELOPE (*pointing weakly*). That man is your father.

PAUL. What?

PENELOPE. There stand the loins from which you've sprung.

PAUL. I don't get it.

PENELOPE. It *is* you, isn't it, Harold?

HAROLD (*enjoying the drama hugely*). Yes, wife, it is. (*To* PAUL) Come here, boy. Your father is home.

PAUL. Sir?

PENELOPE. Go to him.

(PAUL *goes to* HAROLD *dazedly. They embrace clumsily.*)

HAROLD	PAUL
Son, son, son . . .	Father, father, father . . .

(*They part, unsatisfied and confused.* HAROLD *goes to* PENELOPE, *his arms outstretched.*)

HAROLD. Wife, wife, wife . . .

(PENELOPE *struggles to her feet, her face blank.* HAROLD *embraces her, finds himself wrestling with a rigid, unresponsive object.*)

Wife, wife, wife . . . (*Lets go, backs away from her.*)
What's the matter?

PENELOPE (*tearful*). Give us time.

HAROLD. Like hugging a lamp post.

PENELOPE. Give us time, Harold – to adjust to your
being alive.

HAROLD. You were well adjusted to my being dead?

PENELOPE. We adjust to what there is to adjust to.
Perhaps Paul, being young, can adjust to joy or grief
immediately. I hope he can. I will take a little longer.
I'll be as quick as I can.

HAROLD. What sort of time period do you have in
mind? Half an hour? An hour?

PENELOPE. I don't know. This is a new disease to me.

HAROLD. Disease?

PENELOPE. Situation.

HAROLD. This reunion isn't what I imagined it would be.

PENELOPE. A telegram – a phone call might have helped.

HAROLD. Seemed the most honest way to begin life
together again – natural, unrehearsed.

PENELOPE. Well – enjoy the natural, honest, unrehearsed
result – surgical shock.

HAROLD. You feel that you're behaving as a woman
should?

PENELOPE. Every fuse in my nervous system has been
blown.

(*Lion doorbell roars.*)
Who's that? Teddy Roosevelt?

(PAUL *answers the door, admits* WOODLY.)

WOODLY (*to* PAUL). Safe and sound, I see. (*To* HAROLD)
Oh – you came back.

HAROLD. I came back.

PENELOPE. You *know* each other?

WOODLY. We met here earlier this evening.

PENELOPE. How neat. How keen.

HAROLD. How was the emergency, Doctor? Profitable, I hope.

WOODLY. A policeman delivered the baby in a taxicab.

HAROLD. Tough luck. You'll have to split the fee.

WOODLY (*puzzled by* PENELOPE'*s mood*). Are – are you *crying*, Penelope?

HAROLD. She's crying because she's so happy.

PENELOPE. That's why I'm crying.

PAUL. Dr Woodly? (*Indicating* HAROLD) You know who this is?

WOODLY. I didn't get his name. A friend of your father?

PAUL. He isn't any friend of Father.

WOODLY. He isn't?

PAUL. He *is* my father.

WOODLY. No!

PENELOPE. Eeeeeeeeeeee-*yup*. Dr Woodly – I would like you to meet Harold, my husband. Harold, this is Dr Woodly, my fiancé.

(*She crosses to the door of the master bedroom, kissing each male lightly as she passes.*)

Good night, dear. Good night, dear. (*She stands in the doorway.*) Stay or go, talk or sulk, laugh or cry – as you wish. Do whatever seems called for. My mind is gone. Good night. (*She exits into bedroom, closes the door firmly, locks it audibly.*)

WOODLY (*dazedly*). I feel the same way. What next?

HAROLD. What next? You leave promptly, of course. There is no question as to whose home this is –

WOODLY. None.

HAROLD. Whose son this is, whose wife that is. A fiancé is the most ridiculous appurtenance this household could have at this time. Good night.

WOODLY (*crushed, without any possible comeback*). Good night.

(*He exits through the front door*, HAROLD *goes*

at once to PENELOPE's *door, tries it, finds it locked.*)

HAROLD. Penelope! God damn it! Penelope! (*He considers kicking down the door, thinks better of this, turns away.*) Wants to fix up her make-up, no doubt.

PAUL. Is Looseleaf Harper alive?

HAROLD. Alive and hale. He's throwing a little surprise party for his own family. Is your mother often this unstable? (*Not waiting for an answer, calling again*) Penelope!

PAUL. She's a real heavy sleeper sometimes.

HAROLD. Why don't you go to bed – son.

PAUL. I can't take my eyes off you.

HAROLD. Tomorrow's another day.

PAUL. You know what my English literature teacher said about you?

HAROLD. Can't it keep till morning?

PAUL. She said you were *legendary.* I wrote a theme about you, and she said, 'Your father is a legendary hero out of the Golden Age of Heroes.'

HAROLD. That's nice. You thank her for me. Go to bed and get lots of sleep, and then you thank her in the morning.

PAUL. Tomorrow's Saturday. Anyway, she's dead.

HAROLD. Penelope!

PAUL. She was killed in the park two months ago – in the daytime.

HAROLD. Penelope!

PAUL. She was on her way home from a meeting of the African Violet Society, and they got her.

HAROLD (*sharply*). Will you go to bed?

PAUL (*stung*). Yes, sir. If you can't wake Mom up, I've got double-decker bunks.

HAROLD (*stamping his foot*). Scat!

(PAUL *exits hastily down the corridor to his room.*

HAROLD *goes to* PENELOPE's *door, attempts to woo her through it.*)

Penelope – darling – can you hear me? Wife – you know what kept me alive all these fevered, swampy, nightmare years? Your heavenly face, Penelope, my wife – shimmering before me, coaxing me up from my knees, begging me to stagger one step closer to home. Has love ever reached so far? Has love ever overcome more hardships than mine?

(*Silence.*)

Has love ever asked more manliness of a man, more womanliness of a woman? Has ever a man done more for a woman's reward?

(*The bedroom door opens, revealing* PENELOPE.)

PENELOPE (*hollowly, to the world at large*). There is no one in here of any earthly use to anyone tonight. Tomorrow is another day. (*She closes the door and locks it.*)

HAROLD (*to audience*). End of Act One.

(*Blackout.*)

ACT TWO

SCENE ONE

Darkness. PAUL, *alone in the living room, hammers on his mother's door. He wears pyjamas.*

PAUL. Mom! Mother! Mom!
  (*Toilet flushes. Lights come up on the living-room. It is morning.*)
  Dad's got jungle fever, Mom. What'll I do? Mom!
HAROLD (*a moment of exhaustion*). Damn!
PAUL. Mom?
  (*Door to the master bedroom suite opens.* PENELOPE *appears in the doorway. She has decided during an almost sleepless night that she owes it to* PAUL *and to her own self-respect to explore the possibility of beginning her life with* HAROLD *anew. She is terrified of him. She hopes that if she can keep calm and open her fears will diminish. Perhaps she can love him again.*)
PENELOPE (*attempting to behave mechanically as a good wife should*). What are his symptoms?
PAUL. Shivers and sweats and groans. His teeth chatter. What'll we do?
PENELOPE. What does *he* say to do?
PAUL. He can hardly talk.
HAROLD (*responding to a last twinge of nausea*). Bluh.
PENELOPE. You'd better get Dr Woodly.
PAUL. Really?
PENELOPE. It *is* an emergency, isn't it?
PAUL (*uncertainly*). Yeah.
PENELOPE. Then get him.

PAUL (*thinking she has made a mistake*). O.K. (*He exits through front door, leaves door open. We hear him knocking on a door, in the hallway.*) Dr Woodly?

> (HAROLD *enters, drained but recovering. He chews on a root. He has slept in the shirt and trousers he wore the night before. He is barefoot.* PAUL *knocks again.*)

Dr Woodly?

> (*There is the sound of* WOODLY's *door opening.* WOODLY *and* PAUL *speak unintelligibly,* WOODLY *evidently inviting* PAUL *in for a moment.* WOODLY's *door closes.*)

HAROLD. What's that all about?

PENELOPE. We thought a doctor might help.

HAROLD. Your old beau?

PENELOPE. We thought it was an emergency.

HAROLD. I don't want that chancre mechanic in here.

PENELOPE. He's a very decent man, Harold.

HAROLD. We all are.

PENELOPE. Shouldn't you lie down?

HAROLD. When I'm dead – (*Throwing it away*) or fucking.

PENELOPE. Paul said you were awfully sick.

HAROLD. I was, I was. It never lasts long.

> (*He hears* WOODLY's *door open, is alert to* WOODLY's *approach, continues to speak to* PENELOPE *absently.*)

The Indians call it 'Zamba-keetya' – the little cloud-burst.

> (WOODLY *and* PAUL *enter.* WOODLY *is correctly professional and carries a little black bag.*)

WOODLY. Ah! You're ambulatory!

HAROLD. What a brilliant diagnosis!

PENELOPE. You know what I want?

> (*All look at her.*)

I want you both to be friends. I know you both, respect you both. You *should* be friends.

HAROLD. Nothing would please me more.

PENELOPE (*believing him*). Thank God!

WOODLY (*pleased but careful*). Well now – what seems to be the trouble with the patient today? A touch of malaria, perhaps?

HAROLD. I know malaria. Malaria isn't caused by the bites of bats.

WOODLY. You've been bitten by bats?

HAROLD. Colonel Harper and I once shared a treetop with a family of bats. There was a flash flood. There were piranha fish in the water. That's how Colonel Harper lost his little toe.

WOODLY. You have chills?

HAROLD. Chills, fevers, sweats. You can describe it and name it after yourself: 'the Woodly galloping crud'.

(WOODLY *enjoys the joke and the blooming friendship.*)

You can also describe its cure. I'm eating its cure.

WOODLY. I was going to ask.

HAROLD. Pacqualinincheewa root.

WOODLY. Would you say that again?

HAROLD. Pacqualinincheewa root. Means 'cougar fang'. Cures anything but a yellow streak down the back.

WOODLY. I've never heard of it.

HAROLD. Congratulations. By crossing twenty-eight feet of cockroach-infested carpet, you've become the third white man ever to hear of it.

WOODLY (*fascinated*). And you've seen it work cures?

HAROLD. Hundreds.

PENELOPE. I'm so glad you like each other. I was so scared, so scared.

HAROLD (*breaking off a piece, offering it*). Have some.

WOODLY. Thank you. Thank you very much.

PENELOPE. I believe in miracles now.

HAROLD. Wasn't that sweet of me?

WOODLY. More and more we find ourselves laying aside false pride and looking into the pharmacopoeias of primitive people. Curare, ephedrine – we've found some amazing things.

HAROLD. We have, have we?

WOODLY. That's an editorial *we*, of course, I haven't turned up anything personally.

HAROLD. Everything about you is the editorial *we*. Take that away from you, and you'd disappear.

PENELOPE. Harold!

HAROLD. I could carve a better man out of a banana!

PENELOPE. Please –

HAROLD. You and your damned bedside manner and your damned little black bag full of miracles. You know who filled that bag for you? Not Alice-sit-by-the fires like yourself. Men with guts filled it, by God – men with guts enough to pay the price for miracles – suffering, ingratitude, loneliness, death –

WOODLY (*off balance*). Good Lord.

HAROLD. I can just hear the editorial wee-wee-weeing when Looseleaf and I start flying in pacqualinincheewa root. I can hear the Alice-sit-by-the-fires now: 'We discovered it in the Amazon Rain Forest. Now we cure you with it. Now we lower our eyes with becoming modesty as we receive heartfelt thanks.'

(HAROLD *suddenly goes to* WOODLY, *takes his hand and pretends abject gratitude.*)

Oh, bless you, Doctor, bless you – oh healer, oh protector, oh giver of life.

(WOODLY *withdraws his hand, examines it as though it were diseased.*)

PENELOPE. He doesn't *deserve* this! You don't know him. It isn't fair!

HAROLD. He thought he could take my place. It is now

my privilege to give an unambiguous account of why
I don't think he's man enough to do that.

WOODLY. I thought she was a widow.

HAROLD. You were wrong, you quack!

PENELOPE. Awful. (*Approaching* WOODLY, *but not
getting too close*) I can't tell you how sorry I am.

HAROLD. Say hello to your mother.

PENELOPE (*fervently*). *Do* say hello to your mother.

WOODLY. I'm taking her to the airport a few minutes
from now. She's going to East St Louis – to visit an
aunt.

PENELOPE. Tell her to have a nice trip.

WOODLY (*moving towards the front door*). Thanks.
     (HAROLD *laughs. This stings* WOODLY *to a cold,
     peace-loving anger.*)
I'm going to have to report you to the Department of
Health.

HAROLD. What for?

WOODLY. Quarantine, possibly. You may be suffering
from a loathsome disease which the American people
could do without. Goodbye. (*He exits instantly.*)

HAROLD. Now that's what I call fun.

PENELOPE. Ghastly, cruel, unnecessary.

HAROLD. You'll get so you enjoy twitting weaklings
again. You used to eat it up.

PENELOPE. I did?

HAROLD. We were one hell of a pair – and we'll be one
again. What we need is a honeymoon. Let's start right
now.

PENELOPE. A trip, you mean?

HAROLD. I *had* a trip. We'll honeymoon here. (*To* PAUL)
Go out and play.

PAUL. Play?

HAROLD. Your mother and I do not wish to be disturbed
for three full hours.

PENELOPE. He hasn't had breakfast yet.

HAROLD. Buy yourself breakfast.

> (*He takes his billfold from his hip-pocket, hands* PAUL *a $100 bill.*)

There we go.

PAUL. A hundred dollars!

HAROLD. The smallest thing I've got.

PAUL. Can I get dressed first?

HAROLD. Make it fast.

> (PAUL *exits to his bedroom.* HAROLD *turns to* PENELOPE.)

Honeymoon! Honeymoon! Say it: *Honeymoon!*

PENELOPE. It's so – so *stark*.

HAROLD. You used to like it stark!

PENELOPE. Just – *bang* – we have a honeymoon.

HAROLD (*beginning to stalk her cunningly*). I'm not going to strike you. I am going to be as gentle as pie – as lemon meringue pie. You mustn't run away now. This is your loving husband approaching. I'm your husband. Society approves!

> (PENELOPE *wants to run, but doesn't.*)

Good! You held your ground.

> (HAROLD *is very close now, but not touching her.*)

Now – turn around, if you would.

PENELOPE. Turn *around*?

HAROLD (*laughing*). I'm not about to introduce to you a jungle novelty. What I have in mind is massage – a perfectly decent massage. Turn around, turn around.

> (PENELOPE *obeys.*)

I'm going to touch your shoulders very gently now. You mustn't scream.

> (*He touches her shoulders gently, expertly.*)

So tense, so tense.

PENELOPE. You shouldn't have talked to Norbert that way.

HAROLD. You're thinking with your brain instead of your body. That's why you're so tense! Forget Norbert. Relax. It's body time.

PENELOPE. I have a brain.

HAROLD. We all do. But now it's body time. Relax. Ideally, the body of a woman should feel like a hot-water bottle filled with Devonshire cream. You feel like a paper-bag crammed with curtain rods. Think of your muscles one by one. Let them go slack. Relax. Let the brain go blank. Relax. That's the idea – that's my girl. Now the small of the back. Let those knots over those kidneys unsnarl.

PAUL (*entering, dressed to go out and play*). Dad –

HAROLD (*hanging on to* PENELOPE, *but knowing the mood has been broken*). Couldn't you have vanished quietly out the back door?

PAUL. A hundred dollars for breakfast?

HAROLD. Leave a tip.

PENELOPE (*suddenly twisting away, having been nearly hypnotized*). I have some change.

HAROLD. Ram it up your ass!

    (*He realizes at once his violent side has severely damaged the side of him which is the great seducer.* PENELOPE *and* PAUL *are straight as ramrods.*)

I *do* beg your pardon. (*Sincerely*) Those words were illy chosen. There is tension in *all* of us here. Something you must both understand, however, is that the head of this household is home, and he is Harold Ryan, and people do what he says when he says it. That's the way this particular clock is constructed.

    (*Lion doorbell roars*).

Sometimes even I hate that thing.

    (PAUL *goes reeling to the door in terror, admits* LOOSELEAF, *who has also been sleeping in his clothes.*)

LOOSELEAF (*walking right in*). I've been looking at motorcycles.

HAROLD. Go home!

LOOSELEAF. You ever own a motorcycle?

HAROLD (*to* PENELOPE). You're right! We'll take a trip. A trip is what we'll take. (*To* LOOSELEAF) I don't want to talk about motorcycles. I don't want to talk about tits. Go home!

LOOSELEAF. Haven't got one.

PENELOPE (*to* LOOSELEAF). And you went home unannounced, too?

LOOSELEAF. I dunno. Yeah! Yeah! Yeah! I did.

HAROLD. And how were things?

LOOSELEAF. Let's talk about something else.

PENELOPE (*to* HAROLD). Alice got married again.

LOOSELEAF. She *did*?

PENELOPE. You didn't even find *that* out?

LOOSELEAF. There was so much going on.

PENELOPE. She married an accountant named Stanley Kestenbaum.

LOOSELEAF. So that's it! 'Kestenbaum, Kestenbaum'. Everybody was yelling 'Kestenbaum, Kestenbaum', I thought it was some foreign language.

HAROLD. Otherwise, how are things?

LOOSELEAF. I sure didn't expect her to drop dead.

PENELOPE. Dead!

LOOSELEAF. Jesus.

PENELOPE (*sick*). Alice is dead?

LOOSELEAF. No, no – shit no. (*He stops short.*) Excuse me, Penelope.

PENELOPE. For what?

LOOSELEAF. For saying 'shit'. Or is that O.K. now?

PENELOPE (*shrilly*). Who's dead?

LOOSELEAF. My mother-in-law. Fire engines, pulmotors, doctors, cops, coroners –

PENELOPE. What happened?

LOOSELEAF. Well – I walked up to the front door. I was still alive. Big surprise. I rang the doorbell, and old Mrs Wheeler answered. She had her goddam knitting. I said, 'Guess who?' She conked right out.

PENELOPE. How horrible.

LOOSELEAF. Yeah – cripes. I never did get any sense out of Alice. She found me holding up the old lady, dead as a mackerel. It was a bitch. You know – maybe Mrs Wheeler was going to die then and there anyway, even if I'd been the paper boy. Maybe not. I dunno, boy. That's civilian life for you. Who knows what kills anybody?

HAROLD. Could have happened to anybody.

LOOSELEAF. First Nagasaki – now this.

HAROLD. How about breakfast, wife?

PENELOPE. Breakfast?

HAROLD (*as though to a waitress.*) Scrambled eggs, kippered herring, fried potatoes – and a whole onion. I want to eat the onion like an apple. Do you understand?

   (PENELOPE *turns away.*)

And lots of orange juice – oceans of orange juice.

PENELOPE. Mrs Wheeler is dead.

HAROLD. All right – bring me a side order of Mrs Wheeler. (*Regarding* LOOSELEAF, *resigning himself to being stuck with his company for a little while longer*) Oh hell – sit down, Colonel. Penelope will bring you some chow.

PENELOPE. That is the most heartless statement I ever heard pass between human lips.

HAROLD (*honestly mystified*). Which one?

PENELOPE (*chokingly*). 'Bring me a side order of Mrs Wheeler.'

HAROLD. She's up in Heaven now. She didn't hear. She

is experiencing nothing but pure happiness. There's nothing nicer than that. (*Suddenly, angrily, slamming a table with his fist*) Chow! Harold Ryan wants chow!

PENELOPE. What a honeymoon.

HAROLD. Honeymoon temporarily cancelled.

(*Catching sight of* PAUL, *whose physical appearance offends him.*)

The boy should still go out and exercise. I have the impression he never gets any exercise. He simply bloats himself with Fig Newtons and bakes his brains over steam radiators.

PENELOPE. You're wrong.

HAROLD. Then let me see him go out and get some exercise.

(*Explosively*) Right now!

(PAUL *goes reeling in terror to the front door, opens it.*)

PAUL (*to* HAROLD, *abjectly*). What *kind* of exercise?

HAROLD. Beat the shit out of someone who hates you.

(PAUL *exits.* HAROLD *pounds on a table.*)

Chow, chow, chow! Goddam it – nutriment!

PENELOPE. We're all going to have to go out for breakfast. The cook quit yesterday.

HAROLD. You're a woman, aren't you?

(PENELOPE *nods.*)

Then we *have* a cook.

(PENELOPE *hesitates.*)

Cook, by God! Cook! You're the nigger now.

PENELOPE. People don't use that word any more.

HAROLD. Don't lecture me on race relations. I don't have a molecule of prejudice. I've been in battle with every kind of man there is. I've been in bed with every kind of woman there is – from a Laplander to a Tierra del Fuegian. If I'd ever been to the South Pole, there'd

be a hell of a lot of penguins who looked like me.
Cook!

PENELOPE. You leave me so – so without – without
dignity.

HAROLD. People now have dignity when frying eggs?

PENELOPE. They don't have to feel like slaves.

HAROLD (*grandly*). Then go now – and fry with dignity –
sunnyside up.

(PENELOPE *attempts to respond to this, but is too
enraged. She exits, making a tiny mosquito-like hum.*)

LOOSELEAF. I dunno, boy.

HAROLD. The educational process.

LOOSELEAF. I guess. You're lucky you don't have any
old people around here.

HAROLD. She was about to get married again. She
locked me out of the bedroom last night.

(LOOSELEAF *starts to laugh.* HAROLD *shuts him up.*)
What's funny about that?

LOOSELEAF (*apologetically*). You know me, boy.

(PENELOPE *enters from the kitchen with a question
on her lips.*)

HAROLD. I should have torn that door off its hinges.
Should have scrogged her ears off. Should have broken ·
the bed. (*Seeing* PENELOPE) What do *you* want?

(*Words fail her.*)

Well?

PENELOPE. I – I was wondering – is there anything you
shouldn't eat – because of jungle fever?

HAROLD. I could eat a raw baby crocodile. (*Turning to*
LOOSELEAF *crassly*) The way to get your wife back is
in bed. Do such a job on her that she'll be lucky if she
can crawl around on all fours. (*To* PENELOPE) We're
starving. Do you mind?

(PENELOPE *exits dumbly, detesting the word 'scrog',
which she has never heard before.*)

She had two lovers, by the way.

> (LOOSELEAF *starts to laugh again, stops the laugh as* HAROLD *glowers.*)

LOOSELEAF. Excuse me.

HAROLD. One of them is the doctor, whose weapons are compassion, unselfishness, peacefulness – maudlin concern.

LOOSELEAF. Huh.

HAROLD. He and his love are like a retiarius. Do you know what a retiarius is?

LOOSELEAF. He's a kind of gladiator who fights with a knife and a net and doesn't wear anything but a jockstrap.

HAROLD (*amazed*). How do you know that?

LOOSELEAF. You told me.

HAROLD. When?

LOOSELEAF. When we were up in the tree so long – with the bats.

HAROLD. Oh. I'd forgotten.

LOOSELEAF. Fourteen times you told me. I counted.

HAROLD. Really?

LOOSELEAF. You'd get this funny look in your eyes, and I'd say to myself, 'Oh, Jesus – he's going to tell me what a retiarius is again.'

HAROLD (*acknowledging a flaw in a manly way*). Sorry.

> (PENELOPE *enters, is about to speak.* HAROLD *stops her with a raised finger.*)

Let me guess – breakfast is served?

PENELOPE. No.

HAROLD. What then?

PENELOPE. I do not wish to be *scrogged* – ever. I never heard that word, but when I heard it, I knew it was one thing I never wanted to have happen to me.

HAROLD. That's what you're *supposed* to say.

PENELOPE. This is not a coy deception. I do not want

to be scrogged. I want love. I want tenderness.

HAROLD. You don't *know* you want. That's the way God *built* you!

PENELOPE. I will not be scrogged. I remember one time I saw you wrench a hook from the throat of a fish with a pair of pliers, and you promised me that the fish couldn't feel.

HAROLD. It couldn't!

PENELOPE. I'd like to have the expert opinion of the fish – along with yours.

HAROLD (*shaking his head*). Fish can't feel.

PENELOPE. Well, *I* can. Some injuries, spiritual or physical, can be excruciating to me. I'm not a silly carhop any more. (*An unexpected, minor insight*) Maybe you're right about fish. When I was a carhop, I didn't feel much more than a fish would. But I've been sensitized. I have ideas now – and solid information. I know a lot more now – and a lot of it has to do with *you*.

HAROLD (*sensing danger*). Such as? . . .

PENELOPE. The whole concept of heroism – and its sexual roots.

HAROLD. Tell me about its sexual roots.

PENELOPE. It's complicated and I don't want to go into it now, because it's bound to sound insulting – even though nobody means for anybody to be insulted. It's just the truth.

HAROLD. I like the truth. I wouldn't be alive today if I weren't one of the biggest fans truth ever had.

PENELOPE. Well – part of it is that heroes basically hate home and never stay there very long, and make awful messes while they're there.

HAROLD. Go on.

PENELOPE (*blurting*). And they have very mixed feelings about women. They hate them in a way. One reason

they like war so much is that they can capture enemy
women and not have to make love to them slowly and
gently. They can *scrog* them, as you say – (*pause*) for
revenge.

HAROLD. You learned this in some college course?

PENELOPE. I learned a lot of things in college. Actually –
it was Norbert who told me that.

HAROLD (*darkly*). The doctor.

PENELOPE. Yes.

HAROLD. And what is his most cherished possession?

PENELOPE (*not sensing the drift of the conversation*). His
most cherished possession? His violin, I guess.

HAROLD. And he keeps it in his apartment?

PENELOPE (*still at sea*). Yes.

HAROLD. And no one's there now?

PENELOPE. I don't think so.

HAROLD. That's too bad. I would rather have him at
home – to *see* what I'm going to do.

PENELOPE (*suddenly catching on, sick with fear*). What
are you going to do?

HAROLD. He did his best to destroy my most precious
possession, which is the high opinion women have of
me. I'm now going to even that score. I'm going to
break in his door and I'm going to smash his violin.

PENELOPE. No, you're not!

HAROLD. Why not?

PENELOPE. Because if you do – I'll *leave* you.

HAROLD (*promptly and emotionlessly*). Goodbye.
    (*Blackout.*)

SCENE TWO

Spotlight comes up on VON KONIGSWALD *and* WANDA JUNE, *dressed as before. They have become close friends.*

WANDA JUNE. We have this new club up here in Heaven.

VON KONIGSWALD. Yes, we do.

WANDA JUNE. We only have two members so far, but it's growing all the time.

VON KONIGSWALD. We have enough for a shuffleboard team. In Heaven, shuffleboard is everything. Hitler plays shuffleboard.

WANDA JUNE. Albert Einstein plays shuffleboard.

VON KONIGSWALD. Mozart plays shuffleboard.

WANDA JUNE. Lewis Carroll, who wrote *Alice in Wonderland*, plays shuffleboard.

VON KONIGSWALD. Jack the Ripper plays shuffleboard.

WANDA JUNE. Walt Disney, who gave us *Snow White and the Seven Dwarfs*, plays shuffleboard. Jesus Christ plays shuffleboard.

VON KONIGSWALD. It was almost worth the trip – to find out that Jesus Christ in Heaven was just another guy, playing shuffleboard. I like his sense of humour, though – you know? He's got a blue-and-gold warm-up jacket he wears. You know what it says on the back? 'Pontius Pilate Athletic Club.' Most people don't get it. Most people think there really is a Pontius Pilate Athletic Club.

WANDA JUNE. We're going to have jackets, aren't we?

VON KONIGSWALD. You bet! 'The Harold Ryan Fan Club.' Pink, eh? With a yellow streak up the back.

(Both laugh.)

We got very good tailor shops up here. They'll make you any kind of uniform, any kind of sweatsuit you want. Judas Iscariot – he's got this black jacket with a skull and crossbones over the heart. He walks around all hunched over, and he never looks anybody in the eye, and written on the back of his jacket are the words, 'Go take a flying –

(WANDA JUNE *punches him in the ribs.*)

leap at the moon.'

(MILDRED, HAROLD's *third wife, enters. She is voluptuous, blowzy, tough – about forty-five. She has trouble with alcohol.* VON KONIGSWALD *is expecting her.*)

Aha! Hello! You're Mildred, right?

MILDRED. I heard you were looking for me.

VON KONIGSWALD. You were Harold Ryan's third wife. Right?

MILDRED. Yes.

VON KONIGSWALD. You want to join the Harold Ryan Fan Club? Wear a pink jacket with a yellow streak up the back?

MILDRED. Do I have to? Who's the little girl?

WANDA JUNE. Mr Ryan just borrowed my birthday cake. I don't really know him.

MILDRED. Thought you were another wife, maybe.

WANDA JUNE. I'm only *ten* years old.

MILDRED. That's what he wanted – a ten-year-old wife. He'd come home from a war or a safari, and he'd wind up talking to the little kids.

WANDA JUNE. Won't you *please* join our club? Please?

MILDRED. Honey – Alcoholics Anonymous takes all the time I've got – and Harold Ryan is an individual I would rather forget. He drove me to drink. He drove his first two wives to drink.

VON KONIGSWALD. Because he was cruel?

MILDRED (*covering* WANDA JUNE's *little ears*). *Premature ejaculation.*

VON KONIGSWALD. Ach soooooooooooooo.

MILDRED. No grown woman is a fan of premature ejaculation. Harold would come home trumpeting and roaring. He would kick the furniture with his boots, spit into corners and the fireplace. He would make me presents of stuffed fish and helmets with holes in them. He would tell me that he had now earned the reward that only a woman could give him, and he'd tear off my clothes. He would carry me into the bedroom, telling me to scream and kick my feet. That was very important to him. I did it. I tried to be a good wife. He told me to imagine a herd of stampeding water buffalo. I couldn't do that, but I pretended I did. It was all over – ten seconds after he'd said the word 'buffalo'. Then he'd zip up his pants, and go outside, and tell true war stories to the little kids. Any little kids.

VON KONIGSWALD. That is sad.

MILDRED (*blankly*). Is it?

(*Pause.*)

I have this theory about why men kill each other and break things.

VON KONIGSWALD. Ja?

MILDRED. Never mind. It's a dumb theory. I was going to say it was all sexual . . . but everything is sexual . . . but alcohol. (*Making peace sign*) Peace.

VON KONIGSWALD AND WANDA JUNE (*making peace signs*). Peace.

(*Blackout.*)

SCENE THREE

Silence. Darkness.

WOODY WOODPECKER VOICE. Ha ha ha *ha* ha!
  (*Pistol shot.*)
  You got me, pal.
  (*Silence. A baby cries. Silence. The lights come up.*)
LOOSELEAF. Go to the *funeral*?
HAROLD. Of course! Not only go to it but go to it in
  full uniform! Rent a uniform!
LOOSELEAF. That's against the law, isn't it? I can't wear
  a uniform any more.
HAROLD. Wear your uniform and every decoration, and
  let them despise you, if they dare.
LOOSELEAF. Alice would be absolutely tear-ass.
HAROLD. When I was a naïve young recruit in Spain, I
  used to wonder why soldiers bayoneted oil paintings,
  shot the noses off statues and defecated into grand
  pianos. I now understand: it was to teach civilians the
  deepest sort of respect for men in uniform – uncontrol-
  lable fear. (*He raises his glass*) To our women.
LOOSELEAF. I didn't know we had any women left.
HAROLD. The world is teeming with women – ours to
  enjoy.
LOOSELEAF. Every time I start thinking like that I get
  the clap.
  (*Lion doorbell roars.*)
HAROLD (*going to the door*). This could be my next wife.
  (*He admits* HERB SHUTTLE, *who carries a bouquet
  of roses.*)

SHUTTLE (*puzzled by* HAROLD). Hello.

HAROLD. How are you, honeybunch?

SHUTTLE. Is Penelope in?

HAROLD. The posies are for *her*?

SHUTTLE. I wanted to apologize.

HAROLD. You've come to the right man.

SHUTTLE. I forgot my vacuum cleaner.

HAROLD. I forget mine for years on end.

SHUTTLE (*suddenly realizing who* HAROLD *is*). Oh my
    God –

    (*Pause.* SHUTTLE *points.*)

    And *you* are Looseleaf Harper.

LOOSELEAF. Hi.

    (SHUTTLE *faints.*)

HAROLD (*crowing*). It's what I've dreamed of all my life,
    Looseleaf! To have a grown man realize who I was –
    and *faint*! (*To audience*) End of Act Two.

    (*Blackout.*)

ACT THREE

Mildred enters drunkenly up aisle, sits precariously on apron of stage and speaks to audience.

MILDRED. Two days later. The afternoon of the day of Looseleaf Harper's mother-in-law's funeral. You got it? Two days later.

(*Pause.*)

You know what happened in *Heaven* today? There was a tornado. I'm not kidding you – there was a goddam tornado. Tore up fifty-six houses, a dance pavilion and a Ferris wheel. Drove a shuffleboard stick clear through a telephone pole. Nobody got killed. Nobody ever gets killed. They just bounce around a lot. Then they get up – and start playing shuffleboard again.

(*Pause.*)

I never saw a tornado when I was alive, and I grew up in Oklahoma. There's this big, black, funnel-shaped cloud. Sounds like a railroad train without the whistle. I had to come to Heaven to see a thing like that. A lot of people got photographs.

(*Pause.*)

After the tornado was over, a man had some film left and he wanted to take pictures of me – to use up the *roll*. I don't like people who go around taking pictures of everything. Nothing's real to some people unless they've got photographs.

(*Pause.*)

Two days later – right?

(*She exits clumsily, the way she came. Silence. Lights*

come up on the living-room, which has become a pig-
pen. LOOSELEAF, HAROLD, SHUTTLE *and* PAUL
sit around a dinner of nearly raw beefsteak set on the
coffee table. LOOSELEAF *wears an ill-fitting uniform,*
which he has rented.)

LOOSELEAF. I told you the uniform wouldn't help.

HAROLD. It helped more than you know. Down deep,
people were deeply affected.

LOOSELEAF. You keep on saying 'deep' and 'deeply'. I
wish something good would happen on the surface
sometime.

SHUTTLE. I can't get over how you guys are my friends.
Harold Ryan and Looseleaf Harper are my friends.

HAROLD. Our pleasure.

SHUTTLE. Eight years you guys were together – through
thick and thin.

HAROLD. For seven and a half of those years we were
heavily drugged – or we would have been home long
before now, believe me. We were saved from starvation
by the Lupi-Loopo Indians, who fed us a strange blue
soup.

SHUTTLE. Blue soup.

HAROLD. It sapped our will – made us peaceful and
unenterprising. It was a form of chemical castration.
We became two more sleepy Indians.

LOOSELEAF (*to* PAUL). So, kid – how they hanging? Or
don't you *say* that to a little kid?

HAROLD. He's a *man*. (*To* PAUL) Tell him you're a *man*.

PAUL. I'm a man.

HAROLD. We've got to do something to make this boy's
voice change. I wonder if we couldn't get bull balls
somewhere, and fry 'em up. (*To* PAUL) Still miss your
mother?

PAUL (*weakly*). No.

HAROLD. You're free to go to her, if you want. If you'd

rather be a woman and run with the women, just say the word.

SHUTTLE. Are we really going to find out where the elephants go to die?

HAROLD. I'd rather go to Vietnam.

SHUTTLE. Would somebody please pass me the catsup?

HAROLD. What you say is, 'Pass the fucking catsup.'

SHUTTLE. Pass the fucking catsup.

> (LOOSELEAF *gives it to him.* SHUTTLE *dumps catsup on his steak.*)

I keep thinking about Africa – and the elephants.

LOOSELEAF. I don't think I'll go.

HAROLD. Of course you'll go! You're going to fly the helicopter.

LOOSELEAF. I dunno.

HAROLD. You're so *low*! Look at that beautiful red meat. You haven't touched it.

LOOSELEAF. Sorry. At least you've got a place to come back to. I don't have a place to come *back* to any more.

HAROLD. All the more reason to go to Africa.

LOOSELEAF. I dunno. You know.

> (*Pause.*)

I used to really love that Alice. Do you know that?

HAROLD. You know her for what she is now – garbage.

LOOSELEAF. I dunno.

HAROLD. She was always a rotten wife! She was against everything manly you ever wanted to do. (*To* SHUTTLE) He was the most daring test pilot in the country at one time, and his wife made him quit. She made him become a life insurance salesman instead.

SHUTTLE. I'd think any woman worth her salt would be proud to be married to a test pilot. I know I would.

LOOSELEAF. She *tried* to like it. She was a very nervous woman.

SHUTTLE. I could tell that at the funeral. (*To* PAUL)

Would you please pass the fucking catsup again? Was it dangerous testing planes?

LOOSELEAF. I dunno. Who knows? You know – you're up there, and you're in some plane nobody ever flew before. You put her into a dive, and everything starts screaming and shaking, and maybe some pipe breaks and squirts oil or gasoline or hydraulic fluid in your face. You wonder how the hell you ever got in such a mess, and then you pull back on the controls, and you black out for a couple of seconds. When you come to, everything's usually fairly O.K. – except maybe you threw up all over yourself. It's just another job, but you try and tell Alice that.

HAROLD. Insurance!

SHUTTLE. You actually *sold* insurance?

LOOSELEAF. I tried. (*Indicating* HAROLD) I sold *him* some. That was the only insurance I ever sold.

(*Hyena doorbell laughs*).

SHUTTLE. What an awful sound!

HAROLD. Get used to it. (*To* PAUL) Back door, Paul.

(PAUL *exits to the kitchen.*)

(*To* SHUTTLE) It's possible, of course, that you'll *die* in Africa.

SHUTTLE. I've considered that.

HAROLD. Selling vacuum cleaners isn't the best preparation you could have.

SHUTTLE. I just want one true adventure before I die.

HAROLD. *That* can be arranged.

(PAUL *appears at the mouth of the doorway. He has something amazing to announce.*)

PAUL. Dad?

HAROLD. Who was it?

PAUL. It's Mom.

(*He steps aside.* PENELOPE *appears.* HAROLD *and* SHUTTLE *stand,* HAROLD *angrily.*)

LOOSELEAF (*openly, cheerfully*). Hi, Penelope.

HAROLD (*to* LOOSELEAF). Shut up, you ninny! (*To* PENELOPE) You were never to come here again – for any reason whatsoever!

PENELOPE. I came for my clothes.

HAROLD. Sneaking in the back door.

PENELOPE. I rang. It seemed like the proper door for a servile, worthless organism to use.

HAROLD. Your clothes are at the city dump by now. Perhaps you can get a map from the Department of Sanitation.

PENELOPE. I came for Paul as well.

HAROLD. If he wants to go.

PENELOPE. You took him to the funeral, I hear.

HAROLD. He'd never seen a corpse. He's seen a dozen now.

PENELOPE. A *dozen*?

HAROLD. It's a big and busy funeral home.

PENELOPE (*to* PAUL). Did you like it, dear?

HAROLD. It isn't a matter of *liking*. It's a matter of getting *used* to death – as a perfectly natural thing. Would you mind leaving? No woman ever walks out on Harold Ryan, and then comes back – for anything.

PENELOPE. Unless she has nerve.

HAROLD. More nerve than the doctor, I must admit. He hasn't been home for two days. Has he suddenly lost interest in sleep and colour television – and the violin?

PENELOPE. He knows you shattered his violin.

HAROLD. I'm dying to hear of his reaction. The thrill of smashing something isn't in the smashing, but in the owner's reactions.

PENELOPE. He cried.

HAROLD. About a broomstick and a cigar box – and the attenuated intestines of an alley cat.

PENELOPE. Two hundred years old.

HAROLD. He feels awful *loss* – which was precisely my intention.

PENELOPE (*moving towards the violin, and, incidentally, placing herself much closer to* SHUTTLE). He had hoped that someone would be playing it still – two hundred years from now.

HAROLD (*echoing, expressing the futility of such long-term expectations*). Hope. (*He spots the vacuum cleaner, probes it with his toe, asks* SHUTTLE *with seriousness*) Do you hope with all your heart that someone will be using this vacuum cleaner two hundred years from now?

(SHUTTLE *starts to answer, but stops, supposing that he is being made sport of.*)

Fifty years?

SHUTTLE. You're making a joke.

HAROLD (*not joking*). I'm interested in long-term expectations.

SHUTTLE (*flatly, protecting his dignity*). It's engineered to last about fifteen years.

HAROLD (*downstage centre, addressing the civilized world*). Things. Oh – you silly people and your things. Things, things, things.

PENELOPE (*to* SHUTTLE, *as* HAROLD *reflects majestically on the emptiness of materialism*). You and Harold are friends?

SHUTTLE (*revealing how mixed and worried his feelings are*). He's the most wonderful guy I ever met, Penelope. He's the most complicated guy I ever met. I can't believe it, but he's going to take me to Africa with him.

HAROLD. Things.

PENELOPE. You feel I've done a dreadful thing – leaving him?

SHUTTLE (*almost hypnotized*). If *I* were married to him, *I* sure wouldn't walk out.

HAROLD (*directly to the audience*). Never mind the condition of your body and your spirit! Look after your things, your things!

PENELOPE (*to* LOOSELEAF). And you, Colonel? Let me guess: you don't know.

LOOSELEAF. I dunno.

HAROLD (*to the audience*). Go live in a safe-deposit box – with your things.

LOOSELEAF. Jesus – I wouldn't want to be married to *him*. You *know*?

HAROLD. What's this?

LOOSELEAF. I wouldn't want to be married to *me*. We're too crazy. You know?

HAROLD. In what way, pray tell?

LOOSELEAF. I didn't like that violin thing. That was sad.

HAROLD. Tit for tat – as simple as that.

LOOSELEAF. You never *played* a violin.

HAROLD. You *did*?

LOOSELEAF. Yeah. I practically forgot. But after you busted that thing, I got to think, 'Jesus – maybe I'll start the violin again.' That was a mean, childish thing – busting that violin. That didn't just belong to Woodly. That belonged to *everybody*. Maybe he would have sold it to me, and I could have some fun. Then I could sell it to somebody else, and he could have some fun. After you busted the violin, boy, and Penelope walked out, I thought to myself, 'Jesus – who could blame her?'

HAROLD. Maybe it's time *you* got out.

LOOSELEAF. *Me?*

HAROLD. You.

LOOSELEAF. O.K.

(*Pause.*)

O.K.

HAROLD. You're an imbecile.

LOOSELEAF. I know you think that.

HAROLD. Everybody thinks that.

LOOSELEAF. Anybody who'd drop an atom bomb on a city has to be pretty dumb.

HAROLD. The one direct, decisive, intelligent act of your life!

LOOSELEAF (*shaking his head*). I don't think so.
    (*Pause.*)
It *could* have been.

HAROLD. If what?

LOOSELEAF. If I *hadn't* done it. If I'd said to myself, 'Screw it. I'm going to let all those people down there live.'

HAROLD. They were enemies. We were at war.

LOOSELEAF. Yeah, Jesus – but wars would be a lot better, I think, if guys would say to themselves sometimes, 'Jesus – I'm not going to do that to the enemy. That's *too* much.' You could have been the manufacturer of that violin there, even though you don't know how to make a violin, just by not busting it up. I could have been the father of all those people in Nagasaki, and the mother, too, just by not dropping the bomb.
    (*Pause.*)
I sent 'em to Heaven instead – and I don't think there *is* one.

HAROLD. Goodbye, Looseleaf.

    (LOOSELEAF *walks around and gathers his things.*)

LOOSELEAF. So long, you guys.

PENELOPE. What will you do, Colonel?

LOOSELEAF. I dunno. Marry the first whore who's nice to me, I guess. Get a job in a motorcycle shop. So long, you guys.

    (PENELOPE *kisses* LOOSELEAF. *Everybody but* HAROLD *acknowledges his departure in some way.* HAROLD *turns his back.* LOOSELEAF *exits, closes door. Silence.*)

SHUTTLE. Who's going to fly our helicopter now?

HAROLD (*blackly, tautly*). What?

SHUTTLE. We got to get another pilot.

HAROLD. For what?

SHUTTLE. For *Africa*.

HAROLD. Do you really think that Harold Ryan would go to Africa with a vacuum cleaner salesman?

SHUTTLE. You *invited* me.

HAROLD. To make an ass of yourself.

SHUTTLE. What went wrong?

HAROLD. We're ahead of schedule, that's all. You're finding out here what you would have found out in Africa – that you are a rabbit, born to be eaten alive.

SHUTTLE. Gee whiz –

HAROLD. It would have been fun to see you drop your rifle and run the first time an elephant charged us.

SHUTTLE. I wouldn't drop my gun.

HAROLD. You're hollow, like a woman.

SHUTTLE. I'm smarter than Looseleaf.

HAROLD. He can shoot! He can hold his ground! He can attack! You're in your proper profession right now – sucking up dirt for frumpish housewives, closet drunkards every one.

SHUTTLE (*close to tears*). How do you *know* how I'd act in Africa?

HAROLD. Look how you're acting now! This is a moment of truth, and you're almost crying. Slug me!

SHUTTLE. You're my buddy.

HAROLD. Out! Out!

SHUTTLE. No matter what you say to me, I still think you're the greatest guy I ever knew.

HAROLD. Out!

SHUTTLE. You – you aren't going to have any *friends* left, if you don't watch out.

HAROLD. Thank God!

(*He propels* SHUTTLE *out the door and slams it. He faces* PENELOPE *and* PAUL, *speaks with malicious calm.*)

Well – what have we here? A family.

PENELOPE. Almost a Christmas scene.

HAROLD. Goodbye, goodbye, goodbye.

PENELOPE. Just one favour.

HAROLD. Money? There's plenty of that. Mildred got the brewery. You'll probably get the baseball team.

PENELOPE. I want you to tell me that you loved me once.

(HAROLD *is about to dismiss this request majestically, but* PENELOPE *cuts him off with a sharp, dangerous warning.*)

I *mean* it! I must have that, and so must Paul. Tell him that he was conceived in love, even though you hate me now. Tell both of us that somewhere in our lives was love.

(HAROLD *experiments inwardly with responses of various kinds, obviously saying them to himself, directing himself with his hands. Nothing quite satisfies him.*)

HAROLD. Testimonials of that sort are – are beyond my range. I don't do them well. (*Sincerely, not liking to fail in any area*) That's a failing, I know.

PENELOPE (*accepting this ruefully*). I see.

PAUL. I don't care. I don't care if there was love or not. That's all right. I'm going to go to my room and close the door. I don't want to *hear* any more.

(PAUL *exits wretchedly to his room.*)

HAROLD. See how you've upset him. He was so merry and hale before you came home.

PENELOPE. How unhappy he's going to be – alone in his room.

HAROLD. He'll play with his rifle, I expect. That will cheer him up.

PENELOPE. Rifle?

HAROLD. I bought him a twenty-two yesterday – on the way home from Hamburger Heaven. And where is the good doctor? Have you two feathered a love-nest somewhere?

PENELOPE. He's in East St Louis with his mother – visiting an aunt.

HAROLD. Last I heard, his mother was going alone.

PENELOPE. He's *afraid* of you, Harold. He knew you'd want to fight him. He doesn't know anything about fighting. He *hates* pain.

HAROLD. And you, a supposedly healthy woman, do not detest him for his cowardice?

PENELOPE. It seems highly intelligent to me.

HAROLD. What kind of a country has this become? The men wear beads and refuse to fight – and the women *adore* them. America's days of greatness are over. It has drunk the blue soup.

PENELOPE. Blue soup?

HAROLD. An Indian narcotic we were forced to drink. It put us in a haze – a honey-coloured haze which was lavender around the edge. We laughed, we sang, we snoozed. When a bird called, we answered back. Every living thing was our brother or our sister, we thought. Looseleaf stepped on a cockroach six inches long, and we cried. We had a funeral that went on for five days – for the *cockroach*! I sang 'Oh Promise Me'. Can you imagine? Where the hell did I ever learn the words to 'Oh Promise Me'? Looseleaf delivered a lecture on maintenance procedures for the hydraulic system of a B-36. All the time we were drinking more blue soup, more blue soup! Never stopped drinking blue soup. Blue soup all the time. We'd go out after food in that honey-coloured haze, and everything that was edible had a penumbra of lavender.

PENELOPE. Sounds quite beautiful.

HAROLD (*angered*). *Beautiful*, you say? It wasn't life, it wasn't death – it wasn't anything! (*Anger still mounting*) Beautiful? Seven years gone – (*Snapping his fingers*) like that, like *that*! Seven years of silliness and random dreams! Seven years of nothingness, when there could have been so *much*!

PENELOPE. Like what?

HAROLD (*becoming dangerously physical, seizing a battle-axe*). Action! Interaction! Give and take! Challenge and response! (*He splits a coffee table with the axe.*)

PAUL (*rushing in with his .22 rifle at a high port arms*). Mom?

HAROLD. What's this?

   (PAUL *wilts instantly, attempts to make his rifle inconspicuous, harmless, meaningless.*)

   What's this?

PAUL. Nothing.

HAROLD. That's a *rifle* you have?

PAUL. No.

HAROLD. Of course it is. Is it loaded?

PAUL. No.

HAROLD. Open the bolt!

   (PAUL *obeys. A cartridge pops out.*)

   That's a cartridge, if I'm not mistaken. Gunpowder, bullet, cartridge case, and fulminate of mercury percussion cap – all set to go.

PAUL. I was cleaning it.

HAROLD. Pick up that cartridge and slip it back into the chamber – where it belongs.

PAUL. Gee whiz, Dad –

HAROLD. Welcome to manhood, you little sparrowfart! Load that gun!

PAUL (*bleatingly*). Dad –

HAROLD. Too late! It's man to man now. Protecting your mother from me, are you? Protect her!

PENELOPE. He's a child!

HAROLD. With an iron penis three feet long. Load it, boy.

PENELOPE. You're begging him to *kill* you?

HAROLD. If he thinks he's man enough.

PENELOPE (*amazed by sudden insight*). That's really what you want. You become furious when people won't make you dead.

HAROLD. I'm teaching my son to be a man.

PENELOPE. So he can kill you. You hate your own life that much. You beg for a hero to kill you.

HAROLD. I plan to live one hundred years!

PENELOPE. No you don't.

HAROLD. If that's the case – what's to prevent my killing myself?

PENELOPE. *Honour*, I suppose.

HAROLD. What a handsome word.

PENELOPE (*wonderingly*). But it's all balled up in your head with death. The highest honour is death. When you talk of these animals, one by one, you don't just talk of killing them. You *honoured* them with death. Harold – it is not honour to be killed.

HAROLD. If you've lived a good life, fought well –

PENELOPE. It's still just death, the absence of life – no honour at all. It's worse than the blue soup by far – that nothingness. To you, though, it's the honour that crowns them all.

HAROLD. May I continue with the rearing of my son? (*To* PAUL) Load that gun!

(PAUL *shakes his head.*)

Load it!

(PAUL *refuses.*)

Then *speak*, by God! Can you fight with words?

PAUL. I don't want to fight you.

HAROLD. Get mad! Tell me you don't like the way I treat your mother! Tell me you wish I'd never come home!

PAUL (*weakly*). It's your house, Dad.

HAROLD (*throwing up his hands*). Everybody simply *evaporates*! (*Including the audience, inviting it to share his indignation*) There are great issues to be fought out here – or to be argued, at least. The enemy, the champion of all who oppose me, is in East St Louis with his mother and his aunt! I have so far done battle with a woman and a child and a violin.

PENELOPE. The old heroes are going to have to get used to this, Harold – the new heroes who refuse to fight. They're trying to save the planet. There's no time for battle, no point to battle any more.

HAROLD. I feel mocked, insulted, with no sort of satisfaction in prospect. We don't have to fight with steel. I can fight with words. I'm not an inarticulate ape, you know, who grabs a rock for want of a vocabulary. Call him up in East St Louis, Penelope. Tell him to come here.

PENELOPE. No.

HAROLD (*emptily, turning away*). *No*. (*Pause. He contemplates* PAUL.) And my son, the only son of Harold Ryan – he's going to grow up to be a vanisher, too?

PENELOPE. I don't know. I hope he never hunts. I hope he never kills another human being.

HAROLD (*to* PAUL, *quietly*). You hope this, too?

PAUL. I don't know what I hope. But I don't think you care what I hope, anyway. You don't know me. (*Indicating* PENELOPE) You don't know her either. I don't think you know anybody. You talk to everybody just the same.

HAROLD. I'm talking to you *gently* now.

PAUL. Yeah. But it's going to get loud again.

PENELOPE. He's right, Harold. To you, we're simply pieces in a game – this one labelled 'woman', that one labelled 'son'. There is no piece labelled 'enemy' and you are confused.

(*Lion doorbell rings.* PAUL *goes to answer it.*)

HAROLD. There won't be anybody out here. That's the new style: nobody anywhere.

(PAUL, *aghast, admits* NORBERT WOODLY. WOODLY *is high as a kite on his own adrenalin.*)

PENELOPE (*aghast, chokingly*). Get out of here.

WOODLY. It's really that bad? (*He comes farther into the room, bravely.*)

PENELOPE. You fool, you fool.

WOODLY. Oh – look at the poor, crucified violin, would you?

HAROLD. It died for your sins.

WOODLY. This little corpse is intended as a lesson?

HAROLD. There's a certain amount of information there.

WOODLY. Lest we forget how cruel you are.

PENELOPE (*moving to the telephone*). I'm going to call the police.

HAROLD (*frighteningly*). Don't!

WOODLY. I agree.

(*Closes door.* PENELOPE *backs away from the phone, drifts towards* PAUL, *who still holds his rifle.*)

HAROLD. This is man to man.

WOODLY. It's healer to killer. Is that the same thing?

HAROLD. What brought you back?

WOODLY. The same hairy, humourless old gods who move you from hither to yon. 'Honour', if you like.

HAROLD (*to* PENELOPE). He's a champion after all.

WOODLY. Of the corpses and cripples you create for our

instruction – when all we can learn from them is this:
how cruel you are.

PENELOPE. This is suicide. (*To* PAUL) Go get the police.

HAROLD. Stop!

(PAUL *stops*.)

There's going to be no bloodshed here. I know how
he'll fight – the only way he can fight: with words.
The truth. (*To* WOODLY) Am I correct?

WOODLY. Yes.

HAROLD. I can defeat him with anything from flavoured
toothpicks to siege howitzers. But he got it into his
little head that he could come here and demolish
Harold Ryan with words. The *truth*! Correct?

WOODLY. Correct.

HAROLD. What an hallucination! (*He laughs*.) Oh, dear,
dear, dear, dear. Oh dearie me.

WOODLY. You haven't heard me yet.

HAROLD. You intend to crack my eardrums with your
voice? Will I bleed from my every orifice? Who will
clean up this awful mess?

WOODLY. We'll find out now, won't we?

PENELOPE. No, we won't. No matter how it begins, it
will end in death. Because it always does. Isn't that
always how it ends, Harold – in *death*?

HAROLD. There has to be a threat of some sort, nobility
of some sort, glamour of some sort, sport of some sort.
These elements are lacking.

WOODLY. You're a filthy, rotten bastard.

HAROLD (*pretending to be wounded*). Ooooo. That hurt.

WOODLY. You're old – so old.

HAROLD. Now who's being cruel?

WOODLY. A living fossil! Like the cockroaches and the
horseshoe crabs.

HAROLD. We *do* survive, don't we? You're going to have
to apologize, of course, for calling me a bastard. That's

a matter of form – not allowing you or anybody to call me a bastard. No rush about that. Just remember to apologize sometime soon.

(PENELOPE *takes the rifle from* PAUL.)

WOODLY. You're a son of a bitch.

HAROLD. Yes – well – uh – that's another one of those statements which more or less automatically requires an apology. Whenever you feel like it. It's sort of like turning off an alarm clock that's ringing loudly. Your apology turns off the alarm.

PENELOPE (*levelling the gun*). I'm turning off the alarm. I'm turning off everything.

HAROLD. Ah! The lady is armed.

PENELOPE. I want you to get out of here, Norbert. Harold – I want you to sit down in the chair, and not lift a finger until Norbert is gone.

HAROLD (*to* WOODLY). Whoever has the gun, you see, gets to tell everybody else exactly what to do. It's the American way.

PENELOPE. I *mean* it!

HAROLD. Then you'd better fix your bayonet, because there aren't any bullets in the gun.

PENELOPE (*to* PAUL). Where's the bullet?

(PAUL *makes no move to help.*)

HAROLD. Help your mother find the bullet.

PENELOPE (*to* PAUL, *pointing to the floor*). There it is. Give it to me.

(PAUL *obeys.*)

How do I load?

HAROLD (*to* PAUL). Load it for her.

(PAUL *shakily obeys.*)

Cock it, too.

(PAUL *obeys.*)

Give it to her.

(PAUL *obeys.*)

PENELOPE. All right! Am I exceedingly dangerous now?

HAROLD. The National Safety Council would be appalled.

PENELOPE. Then listen to me. (*Angrily*) You're both disgusting – with your pride, your pride. (*To* WOODLY) I hate you for coming here – like a federal marshal in a western film. I loved you when you stayed away. But here you are now – high noon in the Superbowl! You fool, you fool.

WOODLY. Everything's going to be beautiful.

PENELOPE. You fake! You're no better than the dumbest general in the Pentagon.

   (*Pause.*)

You're not going to beat Harold. You're not going to beat anybody. You're not going to stay here, either – yammering and taunting until you're most gloriously killed. Go home!

HAROLD. She's right, Norbert – go home.

WOODLY. I haven't said all I have to say.

PENELOPE. Out!

WOODLY. I haven't told you, Harold, how comical I think you are.

HAROLD (*hit squarely, absolutely unable to forgive*). Comical?

PENELOPE (*to* HAROLD). Sit down or I'll shoot!

   (HAROLD *goes over to her, easily takes the gun away.*)

HAROLD. Give me that goddam thing! Now get out of here, or I might kill *you*. Who knows?

PENELOPE (*terrified*). You've killed *women*?

HAROLD. Seventeen of them – eleven by accident. March! Move! (*To* PAUL) You, too!

   (PENELOPE *and* PAUL *move towards the front door.*)

PENELOPE. Norbert – you come, too. (*To* HAROLD) Let him go, Harold. Let him go.

HAROLD. Of course he can go – if he'll just go down on

his hands and knees for a moment – and promise me
that he does not find me comical in the least degree.

PENELOPE. Do it, Norbert.

WOODLY. Hands and knees, you say?

HAROLD. And terror, if you don't mind.

PENELOPE. Do it!

WOODLY (*to* PENELOPE, *simply, decisively, unafraid*).
Goodbye.

HAROLD (*before she can protest any more*). Goodbye!
Goodbye!

> (*He bellies and bullies* PENELOPE *and* PAUL *out of
> the front door.*)

Get the police! No time to lose! (*He slams the door,
turns to* WOODLY). You're in one hell of a jam. You
realize that?

WOODLY. I'm as high as a kite.

HAROLD. *Glands*. You're supposed to be happy when
you die. Call me comical again.

WOODLY. You're a clown. You're a clown who *kills* –
but you're a clown.

HAROLD. I love you! Have a cigar!

WOODLY (*ignoring the cigar*). Evolution has made you a
clown – with a cigar. Simple butchers like you are
obsolete!

HAROLD. I'm to be left behind – in primordial ooze?

WOODLY. If you're at home in the ooze, and nowhere
else.

HAROLD. This is going to become very physical. Are you
prepared for that?

WOODLY. You're not such a creature of the ooze that
you'd hurt an unarmed man.

HAROLD. I'm an *honourable* clown?

WOODLY. King Arthur.

HAROLD. You hope.

WOODLY. In any event, I will not beg for mercy.

HAROLD. No quarter asked (*Taking a sword*) no quarter
given.

WOODLY. Don't you laugh even *inwardly* at the heroic
balderdash you spew?

HAROLD (*offering sword*). Cut me open. Find out.

WOODLY. I've struck my blow.

HAROLD. With spittle?

WOODLY. I've poisoned you.

HAROLD (*pointing at* WOODLY *in horror*). Lucretia
Borgia? (*Looking around frantically*) Something I drank
or touched? (*Understanding*) You refused a cigar.
That's it! Potassium cyanide in the humidor! Treacher-
ous lover of peace!

WOODLY. I put a poisoned thought in your head. Even
now that poison is seeping into every lobe of your
mind. It's saying, 'Obsolete, obsolete, obsolete', and,
'Clown, clown, clown'.

HAROLD. Poison.

WOODLY. You have a very good mind, or I wouldn't
have come back. That mind is now asking itself,
cleverly and fairly, 'Is Harold Ryan really a clown?'
And the answer is, 'Yes'.

HAROLD (*touching his forehead experimentally*). I – I
really must congratulate you. Something *is* happening
in there.

WOODLY. You can never take yourself seriously again!
Look at all the creatures you've protected us from! Did
you shoot them on the elevator, as they were on their
way up here to eat us alive?

HAROLD (*blankly, as though in a dream*). No.

WOODLY. The magic root you gave me – I had it
analysed. It was discovered by a Harvard botanist in
1893! He explored your famous jungle for five years,
armed with nothing but kindness, a talent for languages,
and a pocketknife.

HAROLD (*blankly*). I see.

WOODLY. You aren't going to hurt me. You aren't going to hurt anybody any more. Any violent gesture will seem ridiculous – to *yourself*!

HAROLD (*quietly*). Don Quixote.

WOODLY. My violin is avenged!

HAROLD. Something seems to have happened to my self-respect.

WOODLY. And the hell with it. It was so tragically irrelevant, so preposterously misinformed.

HAROLD. The new hero is you.

WOODLY. I hate crowds, and I have no charisma –

HAROLD. You're too modest.

WOODLY. But the new hero will be a man of science and of peace – like me. He'll disarm you, of course. No more guns, no more guns.

HAROLD. Was I ever of use?

WOODLY. Never. For when you began to kill for the fun of it, you became the chief source of agony of mankind.
   (HAROLD *picks up the rifle, considers it, offers it to* WOODLY.)

HAROLD. Here. Finish the job.

WOODLY. I'm utterly satisfied.

HAROLD. You're making a mistake. Obsolete old carnivores like me are most dangerous when wounded. You've wounded me.

WOODLY. More clowning! Don't you see?

HAROLD. We never quit fighting until we're dead.

WOODLY. You'd be killing a friend. Don't you know how much I like you?

HAROLD. I'm going to shoot you now.

WOODLY. No!

HAROLD. My self-respect is gone – and my soldier's honour with it. It is now very easy for me to shoot an unarmed man.

WOODLY. New dignity can be yours – as a *merciful* man. You can change!

HAROLD. Like the sabre-toothed tiger.

WOODLY (*sickened*). Oh God – you're really going to kill me.

HAROLD. It won't hurt as much as the sting of a bumble-bee. Heaven is very much like paradise, they say. You'll like it there.

WOODLY. Can I beg for mercy – on my knees?

HAROLD. If you want to be found that way.

WOODLY. What is this thing that kills me?

HAROLD. Man, as man was meant to be – a vengeful ape who murders. He will soon be extinct. It's time, it's time.

WOODLY. Don't shoot.

HAROLD. I've enjoyed being man. (*He aims the rifle tentatively.*)

WOODLY. No. (*He goes down on his knees.*) No.

HAROLD. Get up.

WOODLY. No.

HAROLD. Have it your way. We'd both be better off dead now. (*Begins to squeeze the trigger, falters, lowers the rifle.*) Can't do it.

WOODLY. Thank God.

HAROLD. Crawl home.

(*He turns his back on* WOODLY, *who stands shakily.*)

WOODLY. Thank you – for my life.

HAROLD. It's trash now, like mine.

WOODLY. New lives begin!

HAROLD. Somewhere in this city. Not here, not here. Tell Penelope I loved her – in my clownish way. And Paul. Tell him to be a healer, by all means.

WOODLY. What are you going to do?

HAROLD. Use the sanitary facilities, if I may.

WOODLY. Leave the rifle here.

HAROLD. I'll put it in Paul's room, where it belongs.

WOODLY. Give me your word of honour that that's all you're going to do.

HAROLD. For what it's worth now, Harold Ryan, the clown, gives his sacred word.

> (HAROLD *exits into corridor.* WOODLY *looks after him helplessly, apprehensively. Silence.*)

WOODLY. Harold?

> (VON KONIGSWALD, MILDRED *and* WANDA JUNE *enter from the side stealthily.* VON KONIGSWALD *pantomimes that his companions are to be quiet and to listen for something wonderful. All ghosts cup their hands to their ears.*)

WOODLY. Harold?

> (*There is a shot offstage.* VON KONIGSWALD *is delighted.* MILDRED *is sickened.* WANDA JUNE *is dazed.* WOODLY *collapses in guilt-stricken grief.* HAROLD *enters from the corridor, shaking his head.*)

HAROLD. I missed.

> (VON KONIGSWALD *expresses disappointment.* MILDRED *covers her face.* WANDA JUNE *sucks her thumb.*)

The end.

CURTAIN

THE WORLD'S GREATEST NOVELISTS
NOW AVAILABLE IN GRANADA PAPERBACKS

Kurt Vonnegut Jr

Slapstick	£1.25	☐
Wampeters, Foma & Granfallons	£1.95	☐
Between Time and Timbuktu (illustrated)	£1.50	☐
Breakfast of Champions	£1.95	☐
Mother Night	£1.50	☐
Slaughterhouse 5	£1.25	☐
Player Piano	£1.95	☐
Welcome to the Monkey House	£1.50	☐
God Bless You, Mr Rosewater	£1.25	☐
Happy Birthday, Wanda June	£1.50	☐
The Best of Kurt Vonnegut Gift Set	£6.25	☐

John Fowles

The Ebony Tower	£1.50	☐
The Collector	£1.50	☐
The French Lieutenant's Woman	£1.50	☐
The Magus	£1.95	☐
Daniel Martin	£1.50	☐

P6481

THE WORLD'S GREATEST NOVELISTS
NOW AVAILABLE IN GRANADA PAPERBACKS

John O'Hara

Ourselves to know	£1.50	☐
Ten North Frederick	£1.50	☐
A Rage to Live	£1.50	☐
From the Terrace	£2.50	☐
BUtterfield 8	95p	☐
Appointment in Samarra	95p	☐

Norman Mailer

The Fight (non-fiction)	£1.25	☐
Cannibals and Christians (non-fiction)	£1.50	☐
The Presidential Papers	£1.50	☐
Barbary Shore	40p	☐
Advertisements for Myself	95p	☐
An American Dream	£1.25	☐
The Naked and The Dead	£2.50	☐
The Deer Park	£1.75	☐

All these books are available to your local bookshop or newsagent, or can be ordered direct from the publisher. Just tick the titles you want and fill in the form below.

Name ....

Address ....

....

Write to Granada Cash Sales, PO Box 11, Falmouth, Cornwall TR10 9EN

Please enclose remittance to the value of the cover price plus:

UK : 40p for the first book, 18p for the second book plus 13p per copy for each additional book ordered to a maximum charge of £1.49.

BFPO and EIRE : 40p for the first book, 18p for the second book plus 13p per copy for the next 7 books, thereafter 7p per book.

OVERSEAS : 60p for the first book and 18p for each additional book.

Granada Publishing reserve the right to show new retail prices on covers, which may differ from those previously advertised in the text or elsewhere.

P1481